Mills & Boon
Best Seller Romance

A chance to read and collect some of the best-loved novels from Mills & Boon—the world's largest publisher of romantic fiction.

Every month, six titles by favourite Mills & Boon authors will be re-published in the *Best Seller Romance* series.

A list of other titles in the *Best Seller Romance* series can be found at the end of this book.

Violet Winspear

THE SUN
TOWER

MILLS & BOON LIMITED
LONDON · TORONTO

First published 1976
Australian copyright 1982
Philippine copyright 1982
This edition 1982

© Violet Winspear 1976

ISBN 0 263 74092 7/18/36

Set in 10 on 12pt Baskerville

02-1182

Made and printed in Great Britain by
Richard Clay (The Chaucer Press) Ltd,
Bungay, Suffolk

CHAPTER ONE

THE music drifted up from the terrace of the country club, and the girl who stood alone in a deep window of the games room softly hummed a few bars of the nostalgic song to which the couples danced. *A fine romance, with no kisses. A fine romance, my friend, this is.*

A faint smile touched her lips and a pensive look crept into her eyes. No other song could have been so well tuned to her present mood, as if the band were playing for her alone.

Bay Bigelow was good-looking, the scion of a well-off family, and approved of by Dina's redoubtable godmother. But Dina had known from the beginning that she wasn't in love with Bay. The engagement had happened, as these alliances between the younger members of the ruling familes of Pasadena had a way of happening. A kind of drifting with the tide of social and matriarchal pressure, not enforced but urged on with all the inexorable grace of the moon itself, until the young man found himself offering a ring and the girl found herself accepting it. Such alliances often had a charm of their own, but where was the breathless romance? Dina wondered. Where was the exciting clash of personality and temperament?

Then again she owed Bella Rhinehart such a lot. Her godmother had taken her in when she was an infant, after Lewis Caslyn had gone broke and there had been wild talk of a stock market swindle.

For years afterwards Lewis, her father, had lived in a ramshackle cottage at Malibu, until one day he just vanished and it was assumed that he had walked into the sea and drowned all his disappointments. Dina had been made the legal ward of Bella, who had taken full charge of her, bringing her up as if she were a real daughter, paying for her education at exclusive schools, drumming into her that Lewis had been a no-good rake who had driven his wife into an early grave and then involved himself with racketeers who had finally led him into the shadow of prison, where he would have ended up if Bella hadn't paid for his defence by one of the best Californian lawyers.

Dina had never fully understood why her godmother had this love-hate attitude towards Lewis; maybe at some time she had hoped to marry him, but the fact was that in her imperiously charming way Bella made Dina feel beholden to her; as if she owed her that extra bit of gratitude for the bounty of a good home, elegant clothes, and the cool reserve that made her acceptable to the Bayard Bigelows as a daughter-in-law.

Dina knew that with consummate skill Bella Rhinehart had implanted in her a strong sense of duty, so that she allowed herself to become engaged to Bay because Bella wanted it. After all, it was a comparatively small return for the safe and beautiful anchorage of the house at Satanita, which over the years Dina had grown to regard as her home. She loved the place, with its rambling garden of orchards and bird of paradise trees.

She could still remember the disturbances of her early life with Lewis, and then the sudden sweet security of life at Satanita. It seemed that the one

6

thing she was most afraid of was being insecure ever again—the very thought was enough to send the feel of ice trickling down the straight spine of her slim body.

The drifting music changed to another tune, but Dina hardly heard it. For some quite unknown reason she felt a change in her mood; a sudden tension as if she were no longer alone. She cast a glance over her shoulder, but she was still the only occupant of the room, with a faint light glimmering on the surface of the pool table, where a few coloured balls had been left in abeyance.

Dina returned her attention to the soft darkness beyond the window, and she was staring out there, lost in her thoughts, when beside her own a face was suddenly reflected in the polished glass. She gave a start, for she had heard no footfall across the rope matting that covered the floor of the games room, and she felt as if something clutched her heart as she stared at that reflected face and saw that it belonged to a man. The eyes, even through the glass, held hers with an intentness that was greatly disturbing, and there was no escaping them, for when Dina swung round there they were again, holding a sort of untamed quality she had never seen before.

He didn't speak and neither did she. He was somehow like the Benvenuti painting of *il tigre* Burton; brown-skinned and hard, with a black moustache and matching brows above the metallic grey eyes. In the silence of that long moment Dina's impression was that a foreign sculptor had made this man and then stood him in the wind and the sun and the adversities of life and allowed them to weather his face into a dangerous attrac-

7

tion. He was forceful, not in the least handsome, but instantly riveting.

'It's a game you cannot play alone,' he said, and there was a curiously attractive rasp in his voice; a certain something that touched her nerves and made her feel menaced. What was it she sensed? A relentless, driving energy ... the restlessness of the tiger at nightfall?

'What game are you talking about?' she asked, and she didn't dare to wonder what he really had in mind, this lean and slightly sinister stranger who found her alone like this, while everyone else was dancing or petting in the grounds of the clubhouse. Where was her charming Bay when she needed him? Probably talking polo with his cronies!

'It could be anything, could it not?' He gestured around the games room, and in his hand the slim cigar seemed to belong so naturally, used to emphasise a point, to punctuate a remark, like a sixth finger only a shade darker than his skin. 'There is the pool table, and another with the Scrabble board laid out. Take your choice.'

'Are you asking me to play?' She looked at him with amber eyes that were set at a slant in her otherwise quiet face; her hair was bobbed and it glinted about her head like silver metal.

'Would you be willing to play?' He raised the cigar and touched it to his lips and the drift of blue smoke played over his face. 'It could be that you have found an opponent who could offer you an exciting bout or two.'

'I don't play pool,' she said in a cool voice. 'And I doubt if you are interested in Scrabble.'

'Doubting me already, and we have only just met?' He lifted a black eyebrow and the edge of his moustache followed that quirk. 'If the dancing couldn't hold you, then you must have come in search of something else. To all things a purpose, whether by chance or design.'

'Do you imagine I was pining for company?' She gave him a look that made her eyes look like golden ice. 'I came up here in order to get away from the crush and the chatter for a while.'

'Good, so you are not a chatterbug.' His eyes swept up and down her slim figure in her dress of cool, lovely Kiangsi fabric, then he let his gaze dwell on her delicately clefted chin and wide vulnerable mouth. In repose a reserved face, but when warmed by a smile a sensuous quality crept in, but right now Dina was unsmiling and half inclined to sweep out of the room, except that she resented being chased away by a total stranger. She had never seen this man at the country club before; his was the kind of face that once seen was memorable, if only for the glimmer of sardonic impudence in those grey eyes that were so much lighter than the rest of his swarthy face. That he was a foreigner Dina didn't doubt, and then because something about him touched her on a nerve, she said coldly:

'And what are you, one of the club waiters?'

Instantly the white edge of his teeth clamped on his cigar and a glittering quality came into his eyes. 'You needed to say that, eh? All evening, I would say, you have been in need of a target on which to vent your—dissatisfaction with life.'

'How dare you——?' Her amber eyes blazed and she could have hit him, a complete stranger to her daring to say things that Bay wouldn't have said had they been married ten years or more. 'Who the devil do you think you are?'

'My dear young woman, didn't you just hit the mark?' Blue smoke from his cigar wreathed about his features. 'I am in charge of the dining-room arrangements of the club; I provide the buffet and the liquid refreshment even if I don't serve them. Tonight I had a little business to discuss with the club secretary and that is why I am here. As you are probably aware, his office is on the same floor as this games room and I noticed you as I was about to pass the door on my way from the club, standing alone by a window, absorbed in thoughts that struck me as being rather deep for such a young woman. I thought to myself that you looked like someone who needed to speak to a stranger, for with a stranger we can sometimes be more candid than with a close acquaintance. Ships that pass in the night, which like most clichés has a certain truth to it.'

He spoke deliberately, in that deep voice with a razored edge hidden away in it, and he made her look at him, into those vital and arresting eyes whose metallic grey was a shield for his innermost thoughts. In a moment Dina's quickening pulse was so perceptible to herself that she felt sure he must have sensed it; she felt attacked by an awareness so extraordinary that she couldn't look at him.

'I—I was very rude just now,' somehow she dragged her gaze from his, but even then she could feel his eyes upon her profile, moving up and down her skin under those darkly lashed eyelids. 'I was lost in my thoughts and you took me by surprise. I imagine you must take me for a shocking snob for the way I spoke, but I do assure you that I'm not like some of the other members who regard the club as hallowed ground.'

'Don't be concerned,' he said, a ribbon of smoke twisting from his lips. 'A man in my business learns very early to grow armour-plated skin and you barely scratched me. Now, *dove'l dolore*, as we say in the Milan from which I originated?'

'I don't speak Italian,' she replied, and she was tensely aware that the moment had slipped from her grasp when she could have gone swiftly from the room and dismissed him from her mind. 'What do the words mean?'

'Where does it hurt?'

Her eyes widened and locked with his, for never in her life had any man asked her that; in her kind of circle it was taken for granted that life was *dolce* and pretty young women the icing on the cake.

'That's a very personal question and you shouldn't ask it.' Her voice shook slightly, and she glanced left and right as if seeking a way to evade him, the pearl drops in her earlobes swinging against her cheeks. Her fingers nervously gripped her chiffon handkerchief and just a whisper of perfume stole from her skin, a delicious Givenchy scent that blended with her look of patrician finish and cool delicacy.

Dina had never been so conscious of her contrast to a man, he so dark that he was bound to be dangerous; she so fair with her amber eyes and the court-page style of her glistening hair.

'I do many things that I shouldn't do,' he said shamelessly. 'Such as speaking to a young woman of the Californian élite. My roots are Italian, attuned to pain, both physical and mental. Yours is of the mind, or should I say the emotions?'

'Is it an Italian trait to be so personal at a casual meeting?' She braved a direct look at him and saw

11

shades of hedonist and hard worker in that dark face, and she felt a certain fascination at finding herself quite alone with a man who was unafraid of the impulse to approach a stranger and speak so frankly. Ships passing in the night. It was appropriate, for she was Bella Rhinehart's protégée, and he admitted that he was in charge of the club menus; they were unlikely to ever meet again after tonight.

'Well,' he murmured, 'what do you read in my face?'

'That you like work, and a little hellfire as well.'

'Yes, I am an entrepreneur and I have several irons in various fires. And what is life without rocks to break, fires to walk through, and honey to taste?'

She flushed slightly at that final analysis, and at once he smiled and there was a sudden dark enchantment to that smile.

'*La belle au bois dormant*,' he drawled. 'No doubt you know French, for they teach that language at the finishing schools, eh?'

'Yes, and I'm no sleeping beauty!'

'Are you not?' He looked faintly mocking.

'And you most certainly aren't a prince!'

'I never supposed it for a moment. More likely *une tour mal gardée.*'

'A tower unguarded?' Dina heard herself laugh. 'That you never are!'

'Perhaps not.' He lifted his cigar and Dina stared at the black sapphire cuff-links against his snowy linen. His dinner jacket was of a dark wine colour, superbly tailored to his shoulders, and Dina knew good tailoring and real stones when she saw them.

She thought to herself: This entrepreneur goes his own way, and he doesn't care a fiddler's jig what anyone thinks of him.

'You're probably quite notorious,' she decided to say.

'You bet your sweet life.' His teeth showed their white edge. 'And what are you if you aren't the sleeping princess—a novice nun?'

'In a dance dress and silver slippers?' Never could she recall having this kind of duel with a man before; a verbal duel that was subtly more exciting than brushing off the physical attentions of a man.

'Some women have the cloistered temperament whether in shantung or a coif. Is that what is bothering you? You cannot make up your mind whether you want wedding bells or your freedom?'

'How do you——?' She paused as he gestured at the diamond ring on the third finger of her left hand. She glanced at the ring with its neat grouping of precious stones, which Bay had presented with his charming grin, and which Bella had viewed with such satisfaction. All at once Dina felt stifled, as if she would have given anything to ride fast through the night in the cool breeze and pretend that she was free.

'Who are you?' She pushed up her chin and resumed a look of cool haughtiness. 'Cagliostro the magician?'

'I am Raffaello Ventura, and there are some people who are permitted to call me Raf.' He looked directly into her eyes, holding them with his magnetic grey irises. 'I don't imagine it would surprise you, honey, that my grandfather was of the *scugnizzi* of Milan, scavenging for a living in the alleys and crumbling courtyards of the *palazzi*. He came to America—he established himself. I am part of that. That is what I am.'

'You look as if you'd be at home among the *briganti* of a Mediterranean isle.' He had got under her skin and a kind of fear of him vibrated through her bones. In every way he was a man— possibly a hurting man, and yet her ankles felt clamped to the rope matting where she stood and she was caught and held by him as if those lean fingers were holding her.

'*Grazie*,' he murmured. 'It takes an innocent to recognise a sinner.'

'You're welcome,' she rejoined, and felt that she had scratched below the surface of his armour-plated skin, as he had called it.

'But only as far as the threshold, eh? If I dared to overstep the mark, then you would step on my clay heel?'

'Have you clay in your granite?'

'Hasn't every man?'

'I haven't that wide knowledge of men. Some could be quite saintly, I imagine.'

'Saints get more of a kick out of crosses than kisses.'

'You would know, of course, being the very opposite to a good man.'

'A man of sin?'

'A man who doesn't let sin or saintliness rule him.'

'What does rule me?'

She let her eyes flick up and down his lean blade of a body, and because she was acquainted with young men who kept fit on the tennis court and on the polo field, Dina knew a male body in perfect trim when she saw one—even though this man was quite a few years older than Bay and his friends.

'Work, ambition to get ahead in your particular

field. You don't let the grass grow under your heels, do you?'

'An assessment hardly in keeping with being called a brigand. They take what they want and scorn to toil and spin for a dollar.'

'I said you looked like a brigand, I didn't say you were a stealer of other people's valuables.'

'What about another man's woman?'

'In that area you would probably be less scrupulous.'

'We are quite alone, you and I,' and as he spoke his eyes moved up and down her slim figure in the soft pale fabric of her dress. 'What if we put to the test your judgment of me—with regard to women?'

'My fiancé has boxed with professionals, *signore*. Would you fancy to have your Italian nose put out of joint?'

A glimmer of impudence stole into his eyes and he fingered that bold Roman feature of his face. 'You are forbidden territory, eh, with a diamond brand on you?'

'You could say that.' Despite the flippancy of their exchange, Dina could feel the undercurrent of real intention in this man's attitude. He wouldn't think twice about taking a woman if he fancied her, and never before had she come up against this kind of primitive libido—certainly not in her dealings with Bay Bigelow. With the girl he intended to marry he was the complete gentleman, though Dina had never let herself imagine what he might be like with a party girl, or some pretty young waitress.

'I—I've never had this kind of a conversation in my life before.' She had thought the words were safe in her mind, but suddenly they slipped out and couldn't be withdrawn. She looked at him in some confusion, and suddenly he leaned forward and she felt as if she fell into his eyes.

'That's because you are an introvert, *signorina*, with many things locked away inside you. Would you like to know some more about yourself—it is always fascinating to have a character reading, and you have given me such a reading, eh?'

'A woman has only to look at you——'

'And right away the worst is assumed.' His eyes were wholly sardonic as he held her without even touching her. 'We Italians have always been considered as racketeers or restaurant owners, have we not?'

'Are you a racketeer as well?' she dared to ask.

'Would you be fascinated, or scared out of your silk briefs?'

'Really!' She caught her breath. 'You haven't much finesse, have you?'

'Only when it suits me, and you have been kept so cool and sweet in your reserved little bandbox that I really feel the urge to offer some therapeutic shock treatment. What if I were a gangster? Would you run away screaming?'

She stared at him, mesmerised, feeling again that vibration of fear in her very bones. How lean and strong he looked; how dark and dangerous. He could very easily be of the underworld, and right now there might be one of those small, snub-nosed guns hidden away in some skilfully tailored pocket of his dinner jacket. Raf Ventura ... his very name seemed to hint at dark dealings ... the Mafia, perhaps, that dread organisation with its roots in Italy.

'No,' he murmured, 'you might not scream, but you'd fight tooth and claw for your honour,

16

wouldn't you?'

'I—I happen to think it's worth fighting for.' Somewhere inside her she felt a stab of pain as she thought of her father, and that taint of dishonour which Bella had made it her business to erase from Dina's life, if not fully from her mind.

'You'd writhe in flames if that cool, scented covering of respectability was stripped from your white body, wouldn't you—Dina?'

'How do you know my name? We've never met before and——'

'And hardly likely to have done so, as we move in such different circles.' His smile was brief, his teeth showing their white edge against that black moustache. 'Dina, meaning witch. So you don't indulge in this kind of talk with your fiancé?'

'As if I would!'

'As if he'd even think you capable of such a conversation,' Raf Ventura said mockingly. 'For him you are up on a white marble pedestal, coolly draped, sweet as petrified honey. Now and again he makes an offering to you, the diamond ring, and possibly the pearls in your ears, but does he ever drag you down into his arms and make you feel a woman to your very backbone?'

'This—this has gone too far——' Dina backed away and was brought up sharp against the edge of the pool table, while he, with a movement swift as light, trapped her there with his lean legs pressing against her, and his hands at either side of her hips, holding her. Instantly all her thoughts and feelings seemed strung on fine quivering wires, and she was looking into brazen, dangerous eyes that were letting her know that women poised on pedestals were not for him.

'No,' he said, 'not far enough. Hear the music, hear what they are playing?'

She listened wildly, but it seemed as if she would never make out the music for the loud beating of her heart. Then she recognised the song, *Plaisir d'Amour*.

'Do you know it—have you felt it?'

'Let me go!' She writhed from side to side, feeling the bite of his fingers into her hip bones, through the fine fabric of her dress. 'How dare you behave like this—oh, supposing someone comes in? They'll think I want this——'

'Don't you?' he mocked. 'Haven't you been pining for a man to take notice of the woman in you, all evening, so that you fled away from the music which suddenly seemed like a romantic mockery?'

'You're a devil!' she gasped, and never before in her life had Dina felt so helpless and at the mercy of a masculine force she fought against and yet felt a compulsion to suffer. If she yelled out for Bay, people would come running and she could say this man had tried to rape her. She would be believed because she was Dina Caslyn, the protégée of a rich Pasadena widow, and the fiancée of Bay Bigelow; a girl who had never been known to flirt and throw her favours around.

Yet, knowing this, she locked her teeth and fought silently with this man whose touch seemed to set her skin alight. She belonged to Bay and her life was securely planned, yet here she was like a quivering arrow in the strong arching bow of a body that was both iron and living sinew.

'Never call me a devil unless you mean it.' His face was close to hers and he spoke the words through his animal white teeth.

'I do mean it! You're outrageous—out to make me look a tramp——'

'Oh, come,' he mocked, 'if anyone caught us like this, then the cool and lovely Dina would have an immediate defence. She could plead outrage and I wouldn't have a leg to stand on.'

'If you know that, then let me go before someone does come in—the dance is almost over and my fiancé will want to take me home.'

'What a very fortunate young man—a drive along the coast road in the moonlight, and then a willing kiss at the door of Satanita——'

'How do you know so much about me?' she broke in. 'I don't know you—I've never seen you here before!'

'No,' he agreed, 'swank country clubs are not my stamping ground, but I have seen you at the Sun Tower in Las Palmas, and the Tower happens to be my place. You have stayed there with your god-mother, have you not?'

'Yes——' Dina gazed into his dark face and she knew she wouldn't have forgotten him had she ever seen him before. 'I—I don't remember you.'

'I was up on my private terrace and you were down by the moon pool, and you were wearing a white bathing suit and your hair gleamed like Mercury's silver cap. I remember thinking that I had never seen anyone quite so—virginal.'

'Please—I have to go! It isn't right, what you're doing and saying.'

'You have stopped struggling,' he murmured.

'I—I've run out of breath.'

'Have you?' Suddenly he pulled her against him, so closely that she felt every bone and muscle of his body, and she gasped, a wild flush in her cheeks as his male warmth penetrated through the fine weightless material of her dress. 'Plaisir d'Amour—Chagrin d'Amour, Dina. Do you find love a disappointment?'

'I refuse to put up with this——' She tried to wrench away from him, but it was hopeless, and it was alarming, to find herself in the arms of a stranger so strong, so uncaring of her struggles. Bay never behaved like this. He had never forced her into a position so compromising. Damn the man, she'd scratch his eyes if she could get at them!

'You're in no position to refuse me anything, and you know it.' He put his face against hers, so she felt the warmth of his skin and the hard line of his jaw, his breath against the side of her neck. 'When I caught you by the window you had the look of a pensive Columbine, and it touched me to the quick.'

'You—you couldn't be touched by anything.' Her heart hammered at the feel of his dark Italian face so close to her own; at the madness and danger he had brought into her life, ruffling the limpid surface as a tiger shark the placid waters of a sunlit bay, its dark fin like the shadow of the devil.

'You have the look of what you are,' now the panic of the lonely swimmer had hold of Dina and she was desperate to get away from him. 'I don't mix with gangsters, thank you!'

He laughed, softly, his breath playing over the bare skin of her slim neck, a honey colour from the Californian sun, but almost white in contrast to his swarthiness. 'I've had sticks and stones from masters of gutter Italian, so there is hardly any impact from anything you might call me, in that sweet and cultivated voice of yours, Dina. I will let you go, when you agree to seeing me again.'

'No!' The word and her heart seemed to leap out of her mouth at the same time. 'Never!'

'Never is too long a time to wait, so we'll just stay like this until your charming young man walks in through that door and accuses me of attempted seduction, which sounds nicer than that other more basic word. Will it be swordsticks at dawn, I wonder, or the gloves on at O'Toole's gymnasium?'

'Damn you——'

'Now that isn't a nice word from a sheltered young woman, is it?'

'I—I should let Bay break your nose!'

'Except that it's my one and only handsome feature, eh, and you are a kind young creature who doesn't like to hurt people. Come, where shall we meet? It's no crime, you know, to live a little before you die.'

'You're blackmailing me, Mr Ventura, which is no doubt one of your many racketeering talents.'

'Then scream, bring them running to this room, let them find you in my arms. I'm also a gambler, you know.'

'I—I don't go in for two-timing my fiancé, so I wouldn't know where to meet you. You're the expert in these things, quite obviously, and you won't let me go until I give in, will you?'

'No,' he agreed. 'I hang on to what falls into my hands.'

'Into your teeth,' she gritted, 'like some shark of the deep!'

'I shan't bite lumps out of you, for I prefer you in one piece,' he drawled. 'Are you very afraid of me?'

She lay very still in his arms, feeling the thrust of his jaw and the muscular grip of his arms. 'More annoyed than afraid. I'm not used to being bullied.'

'Coerced, shall we say? Then pretend I'm an avuncular friend of the family who wants to take you out for an ice-cream. You're a woman, and women are good at pretending. You know that, all right.'

'You're about as much like an uncle——' She broke off and caught her breath on a nervous laugh. 'I'm not that good at pretending.'

'But good enough, I'd say.' He drew his head away and his eyes shot their grey challenge into hers. 'We all need a little opium for the senses, otherwise the things we have to face would be damn hard to endure. A clandestine meeting can be romantic, it doesn't have to be the prelude to a disaster.'

'Like two strangers on the deck of the *Titanic*?' she murmured, for no apparent reason, except that he had tilted the fine balance of her world, making this reckless demand that she meet him and become like other restless, bored women—oh, was that what was wrong with her? Was that why she didn't yell out for Bay and make the scene that would have put a definite end to this strange interlude?

She could end it, and yet she gazed back into those grey eyes and allowed them to mesmerise her.

'Yes,' he said, 'two people whose ship is among the ice floes. Will that make it easier for you?'

'Nothing makes it easier. It's wrong, and it could be dangerous.'

'Life wasn't meant to be all honey and roses. The

sweetness can cloy, the scent can become unbearable—you found that out tonight, didn't you? You ran from the music and sought something out there in the dark—the dark gods watch the angels, you know, and they're quick at answering a prayer.'

'A prayer?' she echoed. 'What do you mean?'

'You know well enough what I mean.' His smile was shrewd, making his eyes seem like slivers of steel in his dark face. 'It's no new thing for the sweet slave to rebel against her chains, and I happened to be passing. I don't believe in chains, even if they are forged of pearls and gold.'

As he spoke he gave one of her ear-pearls a gentle prod that set it swinging on its little twist of gold.

'Don't you believe in fatalism—that which the Arabs call *kismet*?'

'Meaning that if I had stayed among the dancers I wouldn't have met the devil?'

'Exactly so.' His eyes smiled into hers, but there was a certain mastery behind that smile, and a glimpse of that dark enchantment she had seen before. 'You have always played your cards from an open hand, now tuck an ace up your sleeve and dare to cheat a little. It might be rewarding, though of course your conscience will be your lash.'

'You're asking me to cheat on the man I love.' The words should have sounded convincing, but instead they sounded stilted, and she saw the raffish smile at the edge of his mouth.

'I wouldn't ask a woman to do that,' he said drily.

'But you are asking it,' she protested. 'You're forcing me to betray someone's trust in me, and I don't like it.'

'I am merely asking you to share a few hours

23

with me; I am not suggesting that you fall completely off your pedestal, dull as it must be for you, perched up there like some pigeon on a column, longing to spread your wings but invisibly chained —oh, there's no need to protest that it isn't so. That would be an untruth, wouldn't it, Dina?'

'I haven't said you can use my name, and I don't have to listen to your nonsense. It's really amusing, the way you presume to know all about me. Does your Cagliostro act usually impress the women?' Dina tilted her chin and gave him a look of scorn. 'Well, it doesn't impress me. I never did go in for night club acts, and reading people's minds. It's trickery, but I can tell you're good at that!'

'You think I can't read you?' He looked lazy and ran his eyes over her face, tracing her features with a deliberation that she almost felt. 'You have a warmth, though you prefer to conceal it, a defiant touch of the little madam, and a definite instinct for self-sacrifice. You also have a sense of humour, but it hasn't been as cultivated as the rest of you. Come, admit that it has its piquancy, being at the mercy of a man who admits to being a knave?'

'The lowest card at court?' she said. 'The rogue in the pack?'

'Exactly so.'

'And you think I should be excited by the thought of dating you?'

'Why not? It should make quite a change from being the cool princess of Pasadena, to let down your hair and be yourself with a man who doesn't expect you to be an angel.'

'Which in plain language means that I have no choice but to say I'll see you again?'

'We both know, Dina, that you have a choice.

Listen, the music has died away down below and the dance is just about over. You could cry wolf right now, and be saved for your ivory tower. Go on. Scream for your knight and let him rescue you from the knave.'

'I—I can't do that, so let's forget it.' Like a shadow in her mind lay the memory of scandal attached to the name of Caslyn, and she shrank in every fibre at the bare thought of reviving the faintest suspicion in anyone that she might have invited the attentions of this man, whose face and voice, whose every gesture held a kind of sinister attraction.

'Scared for me or yourself?' he drawled, and for an instant he increased the pressure of his hands against her hip bones, and his eyes were like steel across her thrown back throat.

'If I have to get involved with you,' she said, 'then I prefer to do it discreetly.'

'It doesn't appeal to you to be caught *in flagrante bello*—in the cannon's mouth, as it were?'

'No, thanks!' She shuddered at the thought. 'No smoke without fire, you know what people are.'

'So none of the shuddering is for the possible breakage of my bold Italian nose? How crushing. Or do you imagine that I might carry a fine stiletto up my sleeve?'

'I'm sure you're capable of it,' she rejoined.

'Oh yes, I'm capable of it.' He held her slim, straining body to his, and her eyes widened as she caught the double meaning in his words, and in his look. 'What colour are your eyes, eh? That streak of honey-gold in tortoiseshell?'

'Oh, do stop this crazy talk and let me go!' She could feel the panic rising in her again, for now the music had ceased it wouldn't be long before Bay came searching for her. 'I'll meet you, if that's what you want, but please—the way you're holding me—it looks so—so——'

'Intimate is the word,' he said, softly mocking her. 'There is a small bay just below the road into Santa Isola. The place is quiet, secluded, uninvaded by the hoi-polloi—be there on Wednesday and I'll bring a lunch basket.'

'Nun's Cove,' she exclaimed. 'Oh, all right.'

'Is that what they call it?'

'Yes—you know it is!' She would promise to go, but that didn't mean she had to fulfil the obligation, but even as she lowered her lashes to hide her eyes, he lowered his lips to within an inch of hers.

'I shall come to Satanita if you let me down, Dina. That is a promise, not a threat.'

'Damn your eyes!' she said heatedly. 'No wonder you have to force yourself on people—I don't imagine you have many friends, only the sort you buy and threaten. God, why pick on me?'

'Now that,' he taunted, 'is carrying modesty into the realms of fantasy. You know damn well why I pick on you, or do they turn the mirrors to the wall at Satanita?'

And it was then, feeling his touch, looking into his eyes, that Dina was closest to crying wolf. Her lips opened and the cry was in her throat, and those grey eyes watched and waited, with a look in them that was so utterly cynical that Dina knew he would let her call him a rapist and to hell with the consequences. He expected it, as if he had no trust or belief in any living person.

'I'll be there on Wednesday,' she said. 'Dare I hope that you intend to behave like a gentleman?'

'Shades of Elinor Glyn,' he mocked. 'Would you dare to sin on a tiger skin?'

'Why, do you intend bringing one with the lunch basket?'

'Caviare, champagne, and a tiger skin. It sounds like being quite a party, wouldn't you say?'

'One hell of a party,' she replied, and knew with certainty that Bella Rhinehart would be furious if she ever learned that her carefully nurtured god-daughter had let herself be forced into a beach picnic with an Italian *restaurateur*. Something quickened in Dina's veins ... a thread of excite-ment tangling with those fine silver threads that bound her in loyalty and gratitude to the for-midable Bella. From a child she had always loved and obeyed Bella, but surely she was woman enough to cope with a man who had seen her and wished to have her to himself for a short while? They both knew it could come to nothing ... a little taste of danger for Dina, with this man whom her smart friends would call a dago.

Even as this thought crossed her mind, she could feel him studying her, taking in every expression that crossed her face.

'Dina and the dragon,' he murmured, and that rasping quality in his voice was very apparent, a razored edge to the words.

'A while ago you were a knave,' she reminded him.

'I refer to someone else who looms large on your horizon, but we won't argue about it right now. Time is running out.'

'What a cynic you are, Mr Ventura!'

'Call me Raf.'

'Even that, even your name is raffish, isn't it?'

'But suitable for a black-moustached dago, wouldn't you say?'

'Cagliostro should be your middle name.' She flushed as she spoke, for again, so disconcertingly, he had read her mind.

'You called it a trick, Dina, and in a way it is. A trick in my Milanese blood, for having sprung from the *scugnizzi* I have it in me to take advantage of every vulnerable chink in the armour of the *nobilta*. You are like a rare orchid which has been kept under glass, and I can't resist taking you out for an airing.'

'Something which has been cultivated into growth, with no naturalness to me?' She felt faintly offended. 'You have a razor under your tongue, Mr Ventura, and you know how to use it.'

'There was ever in the Italian a liking for steel.'

'And back alley tactics?' she couldn't resist asking.

'Ah, would you prefer it if I bought myself into this exclusive club and swung a polo stick at Wild Plage with the rest of the boys?'

'Some hopes!' she laughed. 'You have to be nominated as a member, and the secretary here is probably the biggest snob of the lot of us. You know that, and I don't see you against a background of smart, lazy people who regard hard work as the eleventh sin.'

'You think I like hard work?'

'I know it, Mr Ventura. It's written all over your face. I bet many a time you've burned the midnight oil while you've pored over your account books.'

'If I'm so fond of work, then how come you take me for a dangerous scoundrel?' His tone of voice was amused, but his eyes were intent on her face. 'Are the two compatible?'

'In your case, yes,' she replied, and never had she felt so sure of anything. 'I don't think it would suit you to use up your energy being a dilettante sportsman. You have to compete in the market of raw commerce and cut-throat competition. It satisfies something in you—a drive, a kick, that other men might get from Bourbon, or a hole in one out on the fairway.'

'How tough-hided you make me sound!'

'You are tough, aren't you?'

'All the way, honey eyes, from the roots of my hair to my fetlocks. Do I scare you very much?'

'Yes—you're ruthless.'

'Even so, haven't you had a surfeit of boyish charm and looking pretty in shantung at Wild Plage? Weren't you wishing for a little *chutzpah* on your angel cake?'

'Girls don't always want their wishes to be granted.'

'Meaning that danger is something a female likes to enjoy in her mind, like the fantasy rape?'

'Yes—you don't spare a girl, do you?' Her shapely teeth caught at her underlip and her eyes ran over his face, so dark and different from Bay's fair-skinned, unlined countenance. Bay was so nice, so courtly, so—predictable. Her teeth bit down hard on the lower curve of her mouth.

'Don't do that, you'll draw blood.'

'It wouldn't worry you—you're more than a little cruel!'

'There are different shades of cruelty, Dina.' He smiled down at her with eyes filled with irony. 'I've never pinned a butterfly and watched the filmy wings shrink closer and closer to the slim silver body. I have smacked a man round the face and broken some of his teeth.'

'Oh—why? What did he do to you?'

'He sold me some tainted caviare, but I shall make sure that what I bring to Nun's Cove will be the very best from the Caspian Sea. It's amazing how very ill tainted caviare can make a person, much worse than shrimp, for a couple of pints of milk can cure that.'

'So you're holding me to that promise, Mr Ventura?'

'As firmly as I hold you right now.' His hands tightened, and then relaxed. 'Do you hear voices coming this way—so do I? I suggest you slip behind those window drapes and hide there while I make my getaway. Did you ever see any of those vintage Alan Ladd and Veronica Lake films?' He smiled, released her, and with a sardonic bow he held aside the window drapes so she could slip behind them and be concealed as Raf Ventura made his exit from the games room.

'*Ciao*,' she heard him say, in his attractively rasping voice. 'Just checking the pool table for wear and tear.'

Dina pressed a hand against her mouth, and then realised that she was checking the impulse to laugh. He was a devil and he had made a conspirator of her ... she just wouldn't dare to see him again, and he'd have to eat that caviare all by himself. If he dared to come to Satanita, then she would deny knowing him. No one could pass the automatic gates unless someone at the house gave permission, so she'd be quite safe from his Italian *furioso*.

'Dina darling, are you there?' It was Bay's voice, and she stepped out from the window enclosure and smiled at him, every silvery fair hair in place, and seemingly as tranquil as a moonlit pool.

'Hiding from me?' His smile was lopsided and admiring of her composed face framed by her court-page hair. He held out her long velvet cloak lined with scarlet silk, and when she stood there quietly so he could adjust it so the high stiff collar enclosed her slim neck, it didn't show at all that her heart was still beating faster than Bay had ever made it beat.

'Shall we go home?' he said.

'Yes, let's.' She walked with him, coolly and gracefully, from the games room of the country club.

Downstairs the members of the band were packing up their instruments, and waiters were clearing the buffet tables. There was a haze of smoke, scent, and a lingering excitement in the air. Couples called goodnight and car doors slammed in the driveway. Reminders were expressed regarding the next tennis match, or golfing game, and Dina heard it all in a kind of dream.

They went outside to Bay's car, and in keeping with the general mood of nostalgia and the Great Gatsby era, he was running at present a Studebaker Sky-hawk, and Dina thought how extra boyish he seemed tonight, with his fair hair combed sleek across his brow, and with the lights of the court-yard catching in his candid blue eyes.

'In you get, darling.' He assisted her into the car, and she felt his eyes skim across her face. 'Didn't you have a good time tonight, Di?' he asked, just a little concerned.

'Of course.' She smiled up at him, and thought to herself that she had had an extraordinary time and couldn't quite believe that she had been pro-positioned by a man who was the opposite to Bay in every possible way. He moved round the long body of the car and slid into the driving seat beside her; above them the overhead light burned with the soft lustre of a topaz, glimmering on Dina's hair above the collar of her cloak.

'I thought you might have got a bit needled be-cause Steve Brett and I were discussing the next match at the Plage. You do go for the game, don't you, Di? I know you only watch and don't partici-pate,' he broke into a grin and his teeth were as well kept as the rest of him, 'but I do sometimes get the feeling that you'd like to play. It's awfully risky, honey.'

Honey. A simple enough endearment, and yet Dina felt the twisting of a nerve somewhere in her midriff, and she heard again in her mind a deeper, more mature voice saying that word and giving it an intonation that was far from casual. A taste of honey, he had said. Rocks to break and fire to walk through ... such tough notions didn't touch Bay's life, for the great wealth of his parents ensured that he was in every way the end result of the great American ideal. Polished, good-looking, courteous, and sports-loving.

'Perhaps even women should take risks, now and again,' she said, quietly. 'If only in order to feel alive.'

'You're alive enough for me.' He laughed as he started the car, and he was too unsubtle to catch on to the deeper implication in her words. 'I guess you're just a mite moody, but tonight you looked terrific, and it makes a guy feel proud to have his very own dream, all realised and wrapped up in the shape of the swellest girl that ever got born. I'm touching wood and whistling—we don't want the devil playing any tricks on us, do we?'

He rapped his knuckles against the walnut panelling of the car's interior, and once again Dina felt that nerve twisting inside her, and his mention of the devil made her shiver.

'You cold, darling?' Bay shot a sideglance at her. 'You women wear such flimsy things, that's half the trouble. I say, don't get laid up with a chill just as we've got that big match coming off and I'm all set to score high for the team. I want you at the Plage, looking great and cheering me on.'

Dina drew her cloak around her. 'I'm perfectly all right, Bay. You know I'm not one of your hot-blooded people.'

'No, you're my snow maiden and I like it that way. Did you notice Lenore Hollis tonight, wearing that conspicuous red dress and making a blatant play for Steve? I reckon he ought to get himself fixed up with young Gayna before that Hollis woman gets him into trouble.'

'Oh, Bay,' Dina couldn't suppress a laugh, 'you do sound prim and proper at times! I thought men enjoyed scarlet women.'

'Maybe, but not in front of their friends,' he said, a trifle stiffly. 'Everyone knows that Lenore plays about behind her husband's back, and I'd give her a darn good hiding if she belonged to me—not, I hope, that I'd ever get tied up with someone like her. She's like a guy who can't hold his liquor.'

'You mean she's promiscuous.'

'As a cat,' he said, turning the Studebaker smoothly on to the coast road, where far below the harbour lay still and silvery under the moon, a myriad lights twinkling on the rigging of the moored sea-craft. This was a stretch of road that curved like a mottled serpent, lifting ahead of them, and then falling beneath the wheels with a swish of silken, precision driving. Bay was expert at everything that demanded good co-ordination ... he possessed a kind of jewelled timing in which clumsiness played no part.

'What if you were like Bob Hollis and loved someone like Lenore?' Dina kept her eyes on Bay's profile as she asked the question, the topaz lighting on his smoothly tanned skin. 'Love is supposed to make us tolerant, isn't it?'

'It isn't supposed to make blind idiots of us, Di,' he rejoined. 'In the first place I'd never be attracted to an over-heated female like Lenore, and in the second place there's more to love than being so physically besotted by someone that you don't care a darn what your family or friends think of the woman as a person. There's no pride in that kind of relationship—it's cheap and rather nasty.'

'And you don't think I could ever be like—Lenore?'

'You?' For probably the first time in his life Bay almost drove off the road and had to give the leather-bound wheel a wrench that brought them back on the undulating spine of the serpent. 'Honey, don't go giving me shocks. You're about the last girl in the world to imitate the antics of a cat on hot bricks. I just love your coolness and that calm grace you have when you walk into a room, so that people stare at you as if you're visiting royalty,

34

and waiters can't be quick enough to wait on you. That's the kind of icing I like on my cake.'

'Angel cake?' she murmured.

'Sure, I couldn't have put it better myself.' He chuckled. 'You know, you are in a rather odd mood tonight, princess. Introspective, don't they call it? I suppose it's tied up with the fact that we shall be married before Christmas.'

'And this is August,' she said. 'We're almost at the turn of the year, when the leaves start to fall and the sunsets somehow grow more beautiful. The pensive season, the leaves and the greengages ripe for falling.'

He shot a look at her when she said that, and the topaz lighting seemed to make dark gold pools of her eyes, and to lose itself in the slight hollows under her cheekbones.

'I've always liked the little bit of mystery about you,' he said. 'You're not like other girls—you're much deeper than the usual crowd. I'm lucky to have you, and I intend to hold on to you.'

Dina's heart gave a tiny flutter at his words and his sudden possessive tone of voice. Silence fell between them and she knew from the shadowy depths beyond the road that they were nearing Satanita. The car accelerated as it began its climb into the higher hills, making for the tall gates that would be opened to the blare of the Studebaker's horn. A tunnel of tall aracaria trees led towards the house, making an avenue of shadow and leafy scent.

The house had turrets like a white castle in the moonlight, and its rooftops sloped and shone like polished stones. The wall lamps in the forecourt cast their dull gold light upon the steps that led to the high front door, and Dina felt a sense of relief that she was home at last from the demands and problems created for her now she was grown up and could no longer think of Satanita as her fortress against the invading forces of adult life.

'I'm so very tired——'

But her fiancé caught at her hand as she went to mount the steps and he held her in abeyance in the bulk of one of the huge, spike-flowered cedars that flanked the steps like a pair of venerable sentinels.

'Were you talking to him?'

'Who——?' She looked at Bay with startled eyes. 'Who are you talking about?'

'That foreign-looking guy who came out of the games room just as I reached the door—I was with Steve who wanted the club secretary to cash a cheque for him. We both noticed the guy, who said something in Italian. You were in the games room, Di. Surely you saw him?'

'I—I knew that someone came in for a few minutes.' Dina hated to tell lies, yet here she was denying all knowledge of Raf Ventura. 'I was in that window alcove and I came out when you called me.'

'So you didn't exchange any kind of talk with him—tall, dark as the devil, and certainly not a club member, otherwise I'd have recognised him. He gave me a strange sort of glance as he passed by—malevolent, I'd call it.'

'Oh, don't talk such nonsense!' For some odd reason she felt a stab of vexation and wanted to pull free of Bay's hand. 'I daresay he was at the club on business. Not everyone spends their life having a ball!'

'Is that a dig at me?' A thread of lamplight revealed the frown that drew Bay's sun-bleached eyebrows into a line. 'If my father was in business instead of being a senator, then I'd no doubt work for him. But I'd be no good at politics, Di. Okay, so we're affluent, but we aren't idle. We keep occupied, and I did my spell out in Vietnam.'

'Oh, Bay, I'm not criticising you, but you, me, our friends, we seem to regard anyone outside our circle as being a kind of—of menace to our way of life. I mean—*malevolent*.'

'I've never seen brows so black, and eyes so glittering, like the sharp steel those dagos are fond of—'

That word twisted the knife and she did wrench free of Bay's hand. 'I'm tired and I don't plan to stand here half the night discussing a stranger, who is probably quite respectable and no more dangerous than you or I.'

'If you think that, Di, then you couldn't have seen him. He gave me the feeling of being marked out, similar to that out in Vietnam when you sensed that a sniper was around and your name might be on the next bullet. I mean it, Di. I know when someone is giving me the evil eye.'

'I've never heard you talk such rot!' Dina gathered her cloak around her and ran up the steps to her front door. It was slightly alarming that her legs felt shaky. 'Go home, Bay, and mind how you drive. I'll see you at the match on Friday.'

'Shall I pick you up, or will you drive down?' He sounded slightly offended, as if he thought she were treating him like a fanciful boy.

'I'll drive down, which will give you more time to prepare yourself for the game. Goodnight, Bay.'

She quickly turned her key in the lock and slipped inside the house before he had time to demand a less formal goodnight. She stood inside the door and didn't fully relax until she heard the Studebaker drive away into the night.

It wasn't like Bay Bigelow to have such fancies ... had he really seen threat in Raf Ventura's eyes, or was that his general reaction to someone who was obviously foreign and not a member of Pasadena's thoroughbred pack?

Dina made her way upstairs to her room, moving quietly, her cloak over her arm so it wouldn't rustle in the stillness and be heard by Bella, who was a light sleeper. Dina felt that tonight she had indulged in enough disturbing talk, and her god-mother had an uncanny knack of sensing when Dina was troubled and she'd want to know the reason. She'd probe and guess there had been a slight difference with Bay, and the very next time she saw him she would worm it out of him that there had been a stranger at the country club ... a dark, foreign stranger over whom they had almost quarrelled.

The last thing Dina wanted was for her god-mother to learn about Raf Ventura, and with bated breath she crept past Bella's bedroom, and she didn't breathe freely until she reached the safety of her own room. She stood there in the darkness, listening for the smallest sound. She almost betrayed the tense state of her nerves when the little clock chimed on her mantelpiece, each stroke blending with the nervous beat of her heart.

Midnight, she thought, and the ball was over. Tomorrow she would be able to talk about the dance quite casually ... in the sober light of day the events of tonight would seem like a fantasy and she would be able to smile and dismiss from her mind that meeting with a man who had no part to play in her life.

Tomorrow it would all seem like a half-remembered dream.

CHAPTER TWO

DINA kept her word to herself and didn't keep that
appointment at Nun's Cove—how could she, after
what Bay had said, and in view of her own subtle
doubts that it would not be altogether wise to en-
courage such a man.

She attended the polo match on Friday and it
was quite exciting, with Bay's team winning by a
couple of chukkas. They and their circle of friends
had tea afterwards in the clubhouse of the polo
field, and it was a bright, unclouded party, and to
her relief Bay appeared to have forgotten their
slight tiff and the cause of it. The day ended on a
happy note, and she had quite put out of her mind
that threat by Raf Ventura that he would come to
Satanita if she dared to defy him.

She had dared, and had half feared that he would
appear in some shining monster of a car at the gates
of Satanita. When several days passed and she
heard no more of him, she relaxed a little and concluded that he had taken the hint that water and
fire didn't mix.

It was true that Bella's large house on its imposing hill, surrounded by several acres of beautifully natural gardens, had gates at its drive that
were firmly closed to uninvited guests, but there
was what could only be called a Judas entrance by
way of the grounds themselves, for their boundary
was a wooded area, so thickly populated by trees
and birds that hardly anyone ever trespassed there.

A rough, pathway had been worn out by the coming and going of Dina on horseback, for the woods gradually descended to a lonely stretch of beach and sea-sculpted rocks. She regarded the place as very much her own, and in the saddle of Major she would gallop in the surf. The pair of them loved the exercise and the solitude; the awareness that they wouldn't be intruded upon.

Not for one moment did it occur to Dina that someone else would use that rough pathway in the same way as herself, coming on horseback into the grounds of Satanita; riding along its avenues of trees and exotic shrubs, planted long ago by Bella's husband, until the clatter of hooves fell upon Dina's ears as she sat in the attractive little *sala* where she usually wrote letters and read the morning papers.

She glanced up from her newspaper and stared incredulously at the horse and rider beyond the long glass doors of the *sala*. Both were dark, well groomed and perfectly at ease. Those deep-set, alive and arresting eyes penetrated through the glass itself and they seemed to bathe Dina in a wave of confusion, shock ... and guilt.

Deliberately, mockingly, he raised his riding-stick in a salute. He wore a tailored hacking-jacket in dice-checks, a pair of equally well tailored khaki breeches, and kneeboots. He seemed to aim at emphasising that dark, devilish quality in himself, Dina thought, and she could feel a tremor in her legs as she rose from her chair and watched him dismount from the glossy-coated horse. She saw his dark hand stroke down the length of the animal's neck and he murmured some words, probably Italian, which the handsome creature would have been trained to understand and obey. A sorcerer's incantation, Dina told herself, and she stood there dumbly and realised how subtle was this man who guessed he would be refused entrance at the gates and so found another way to get in.

Her way, damn his impudence!

That flash of anger brought her out of her trance and she made for the french doors and opened them out wide, with a tempered sweep of her hands. She stepped out on to the flagstones of the courtyard and her amber eyes were blazing.

'How dare you come here! What right have you? This is private property and I shall get Hudson and his dogs to chase you off our grounds!'

'I have a way with dogs,' he drawled, standing there and bending the flexible whip in his lean fingers. 'And I guess that was Hudson I saw as I cantered along here, a sandy-haired man with Scottish eyes. He seemed to take me for a—friend of yours.'

'You're no friend of mine! You're nothing but a darn trespasser! How did you know about that way through the woods? I'm the only person who ever goes there.'

'Cagliostro had many tricks up his sleeve, Dina.' His grey eyes swept up and down her slim figure in a sleeveless dress the colour of jacaranda. 'Yes, with the sun on your hair and skin you are even more attractive than seen under the artificial lights of a dance floor.'

There was something intensely personal about the remark, and Dina met it with a proud lift of her head. 'Don't you know when to take a hint, Mr Ventura? I should think when I didn't turn up at Nun's Cove you'd have guessed that I didn't wish to see you again. I suppose the truth is that you couldn't be expected to act the gentleman!'

'Indeed, that is very much the truth,' he agreed, and into his eyes came that glint that was both ironic and dangerous. 'But is it really all that lady-like to let a man come all the way from Las Palmas, with chilled champagne and a carton of the best caviare, and not even leave a note for him, under a rock, maybe, letting him know that the lady won't be joining him for lunch.'

'Did you really imagine that I would be there?'

'Yes, I did imagine something of the sort—did you get cold feet after your young man mentioned that he and I met eye to eye in the corridor outside the games room? He's a good-looking playboy, but possibly not as stupid as he appears.'

'You've got more damn nerve than a rattle-snake!' Dina exclaimed. 'I won't have Bay talked about in that sarcastic manner—who do you think you are?'

'It isn't a question of who I think I am, for I know the answer only too well. The problem is that you aren't sure of who I am, for you've never met my like before, have you, Dina? Did you really suppose that you could brush me off, and that I wouldn't hold to my threat of coming here to Sata-nita? It's a charming old property. Quite the castle for the Sleeping Beauty, with its own enchanted wood that might keep at bay anyone but a man intent on waking the princess from her trance. I've always felt that it would take a wily knave to break the spell rather than a boyish knight with his golden quiff across his brow.'

'Do you always talk in riddles?' she asked. 'I'm under no spell, and if I ever did need a gallant to come to my aid, I'd choose someone I could trust. Bay did see you the other night and he wanted to know if you'd spoken to me. I had to lie to him, and I don't like deceit.'

'Why do you feel you had to lie to him?' One of the dense black brows rose inquisitively. 'You could easily have said that some foreign waiter had accosted you——'

'Oh, stop it! I believe you're doing this because I called you a waiter.' Dina glanced round in a hunted way, for Bella would now be up and might appear at any moment, and it would be reasonable if she wanted to be introduced to this unexpected caller. Even in his tailored riding clothes he still looked utterly foreign, and the black moustache that curved down over his upper lip gave him an added air of diablerie. Bella would be far from pleased to make his acquaintance, especially when she learned that his only connection with the country club set was in the capacity of providing 'fodder and drink' for the members.

'I do wish you'd go,' she said. 'My godmother won't like it if she finds out you came here unin-vited. She keeps a strict eye on the coming and going of visitors, for there are valuable antiques in the house.'

'Really?' he drawled, and his eyes were infinitely mocking as they dwelt on Dina's tense face. 'I do assure you, Miss Caslyn, that I have no interest whatsoever in anything of antique value in your godmother's imposing house. In fact, I'm rather looking forward to meeting the lady.'

'You can't possibly do that! If you're hoping to crash your way into Pasadena society by way of meeting Bella, then you can think again. I can assure you that *restaurateurs* are not on her visiting list.'

'I'm quite certain of that.' Not a fraction of his self-assurance had been dented by Dina's crushing remarks, and that glint of impudence was still there in his grey eyes. 'I can candidly say right this moment that the very last thing I want is to crash my way into the kind of society ruled over by formidable and snobbish old ladies whose main aim in life is to preserve the *status quo* of the middle classes, many of whom have grand houses and a secure income based on the mercenary dealings of ancestors outlawed from their homelands for various petty crimes, and packed off to colonial countries in bond to farmers and factory owners, whom they no doubt conned with such expertise that in no time at all they became the bosses. I quite admire their shrewdness and industry, but that doesn't make me feel subservient to your kind, Dina. I'd want no part of such a society if it were handed to me on a golden plate and fed to me from a jewelled spoon.'

'Then what are you doing here?' Dina wanted to know. 'If you despise my background so much, then what are you after?'

'Retribution,' he replied, and with the barest movement of his wrist he sent the lash of his whip curling around her waist. She gasped as she felt it biting into her and was compelled to move in his direction as he pulled on the whip. 'I come of a people, Dina, to whom the vendetta is as much of a driving force in the blood as the acquisition of wealth and privilege is in the bones of your breed.'

'You're doing this to me just because I didn't keep that rendezvous at Nun's Cove?' She spoke

45

indignantly and tried not to let the panic show that he had her firmly secured by his whip.

'The trick is to handle a woman or a horse without marking the skin,' he drawled, sensing her panic even as she fought not to show it. 'Why shouldn't I demand retribution for being let down?'

'Why, aren't you used to it?' She gave a scornful toss of her head. 'Do women usually obey your slightest demand and leap to do your bidding when you crack your whip? I suppose it must have come as a blow when I failed to show up. Did you fondly imagine that I would be there?'

'I was led to believe that young women who've been nurtured like hothouse blooms have courtesy among their virtues, but it would seem that I was mistaken.'

'So it counts as a crime if a woman dares to show you a little discourtesy? Really, Mr Ventura, you don't look that thin-skinned. In fact, I'd say you were one of the toughest men I'd ever met.'

'Even the toughest have their vulnerable moments. I was exceedingly piqued at having to lunch alone when I had expected company. I had to feed half the caviare to the fishes, and champagne lacks sparkle when there isn't a woman to share it, especially a haughty, honey-eyed little blonde. I warned you not to break that date, didn't I? I said I'd come to Satanita and you obviously thought that the guarded gates of the fortress would keep me out. A wily brigand never attacks from the front when from the rear he can take the fort without firing a shot.'

'I suppose that's how you've succeeded in business, you find out the weak place, the chink in the armour, and you take your competitors and opponents by surprise. You're a dangerous man, aren't you, Mr Ventura?'

'I hope I am,' he drawled. 'Men without any danger in them must be as bland as apple pie without cloves; as a tiger without teeth. The unpredictable elements in life are surely more exciting than those we can predict? It's in the nature of the human animal, that need to feel the adrenalin pumping through the veins. Without that we'd be figures of wax and fixed attitudes.'

The annoying fact for Dina was that she found herself agreeing with what he said, but nothing short of torture would have made her admit it. He was a tiger, all right, and he had a set of strong white teeth that had clamped themselves in the scruff of life and given it a powerful shake.

Her eyes raced over his face and saw there the subtlety and strength that made him so different from young, smooth men like Bay who had not had to stalk their fortunes through the jungles of trade and commerce. The tiger analogy was very close to the skin of Raf Ventura; he moved with the lithe, noiseless gait of the jungle's most wily inmate; his reactions would be equally alert, his attack just as swift and deadly.

Dina felt a strong sense of antagonism towards him, and yet she couldn't have said that his looks, his voice, or his manner of dressing were repellent to her. He made her feel unsure of herself; he disproved the theory that men and women were only persons ... she was unbearably aware of being a female whom this particular male could have rendered senseless with an uppercut and carried off into the depths of the garden. His toughness of

body extended to his feelings, she was sure of that
... he was also a self-made man who didn't like
being given the brush-off by a socialite, and Dina
supposed that she came under that heading as the
goddaughter of one of Pasadena's wealthiest, most
prominent women.

Yes, that was how he'd regard her, unaware that
she could gaze down the years to a time of shadow,
when she had been too young to understand why
she came to live with Bella and why her father
lived like a beachcomber ... until he suddenly dis-
appeared and there were whispers about suicide ...
or a shark off-shore.

With a sudden, unexpected jerk of the whip he
brought her right against him. 'Cool as ice, aren't
you?' he said. 'Sure of your place and the life you
plan to live with your nice young man.'

'Why not?' she said, giving him a defiant look
even as she felt the hammering of her heart, and a
physical dominance never encountered in her life
before. 'I shan't be marrying a tame man, even if
you think he is. Bay was out in Vietnam—he hasn't
gone through life without facing danger. While he
was fighting you were probably serving pheasant
flambé!'

'I was serving all right,' he drawled. 'I flew heli-
copters over the battle areas and I had to pick up
those wounded beyond our own lines—oh yes, I
saw quite a few cases of flaming carcase, Miss
Caslyn.'

Dina caught her breath and realised that in
terms of years he was not all that much older than
Bay Bigelow, he only looked as if he had lived a
decade more than Bay.

'Say you're sorry,' he ordered. 'Just because I

don't come out of the same smooth mould as your boy-friends, that doesn't mean that I'm creaking with age. How old did you think I was?'

'I—I hadn't given it a moment's thought. Your age is nothing to me—why should it be?'

'Because spring and winter just don't mix. I'm thirty-six, to be exact; my birthday was on Wednesday and my party just wasn't what I'd hoped it would be.'

'Oh——' Dina flushed slightly, and wished he didn't have such a knack for taking her by surprise. 'I'm sorry about that, but you might have guessed that I wouldn't be there. I don't play around behind my fiancé's back—he's much too nice.'

'Nice?' Raf Ventura raised a black eyebrow. 'Is that all you're asking from life, for a nice boy to fit you into his schedule that's crowded with polo matches, golf tournaments, and tennis bouts? Are you so scared of a full relationship with a man that you actually welcome the idea of playing fourth fiddle in his orchestra of sporting activities? When do you suppose he'll have the time or the energy for you?'

'Oh—how dare you say such a thing!' Sheer blazing anger flashed through Dina and she raised a hand and struck at him, hating him, a stranger, for raking up what had lain at the root of her own pensive, almost lonely feeling the night this man had walked into her life. His facial bones felt hard under the impact of her hand, and she heard the slap and saw his lips twist into a mordaunt smile under the black edge of his moustache.

'Does the truth have to be nicely dressed before it's served up, Miss Caslyn, like everything else in your world? Don't you people like to know that the turtles are stewed alive before the soup comes to your table; that certain cats and other creatures suffer the torments of the damned so you can hide your basic humanity in a cloud of scent and soft furs? Can you honestly say that you haven't longed at times to join the human race?'

'Shut up!' She shivered in the sunshine that came slanting through the trees and across his face, making his eyes seem like darkly burning steel. 'I didn't ask for this, to have my thoughts and feelings speared out of me—by you! What have I done to you?'

'Had the temerity to get under my skin, perhaps. I look at you, Dina, and realise how sweet vengeance might be.'

'Revenge is an evil thing,' she said, in a strained voice. 'We're supposed to turn the other cheek.'

'Then I'll turn it, Dina, and you can slap me a second time—only I warn you that you may bring out the devil in me.' He turned his head mockingly, and she ran her eyes wildly up and down that hard-boned profile, with deep lines incised in the dark skin. It was an incredibly Roman profile, as if stamped in weathered bronze ... one of those coins from old tombs, with a mysterious significance to it. When she didn't speak, he lowered his voice until it was softly grating against her ear.

'It's traditional for the devil to call on Eve in her garden. Aren't you tempted ... with me you can speak the painful truth. You don't have to spare my sensitive feelings with a soft lie.'

'I—I thought you were threatening me, but now you speak of temptation.' Despite the fear, the edgy panic, the resentment of the way he had come here, riding through the grounds of Satanita like some swarthy figure of Latin vengeance, Dina spoke bravely enough. It was a defiant kind of bravery, like that she displayed when out with the Pasadena hunting pack, with those blood-lusting hounds racing in for the kill. She hunted because Bella expected her protégée to do so, but no one knew how desperately Dina hated the savagery of it, and how much she was on the side of the vixen. She cheered inwardly when the vixen went to earth and evaded the hounds, even as she maintained a look of cool disinterest; a look which she tried to maintain in the face of Raf Ventura.

'The idea of tempting you, Dina, is far more intriguing than any threat could be. I wonder,' his eyes moved deliberately over her face, 'if you fully realise the impact that your cool air of chastity has on a man?'

'It would doubtless appeal to you, Mr Ventura, to want to drag my sort through the mud,' she retorted. 'Will that satisfy your urge for vengeance, to make me look cheap? Is that what you're hoping to do? Then I'll walk into the sea before you do it—you won't drag me down!'

'It isn't that easy to die, honey, and I speak from the experience of seeing men survive injuries like nothing you could ever imagine.'

'Walking into the sea is different,' she said, and the distant shadow of her father's disappearance was there in her eyes.

'Maybe for someone who can't swim,' he said, and he was looking down at her with narrowed eyes, glittering under his lowered lids. 'I know you can because I saw you in the pool at my Sun Tower, but when people are lost in the sea there is usually a good reason, such as a killer shark in the mood for an attack.'

'Oh God,' Dina gave a shudder, 'do you have to be so graphic?'

'Yes, if I'm going to prove to you that dying is as difficult as living, and often a lot more painful.' He looked downwards into the expanded pupils of her eyes, as if seeing there his own lean and rather merciless face. 'I watched you unobserved during that week you stayed at my hotel, cool-skinned, reserved, the perfect little lady reared by Bella Rhinehart to make the perfect marriage with the son of a Senator. How very different our two lives have been, for I've worked my way up from dishwasher to food carrier, to laying the tables and then serving the clients. I have no regrets for the way I've worked and schemed, for in the end I achieved my goals—all but one.'

He smiled with just a brief movement of his lips—well-cut lips above the clean definition of his jaw, with not a hint of self-indulgence but with definite shadings of a determined and ruthless man.

'On a table in that charming little room I see a coffee pot,' he said. 'Is there a chance that it's still warm, and may I beg a cup?'

'You've never begged for anything,' she replied, and then realised that if she agreed to give him a cup of coffee he would have to release her from the imprisonment of his whip. It seemed almost inevitable that Bella would soon appear, and if her confrontation with Raf Ventura had to take place, then it would be infinitely better if her godmother didn't find her like this ... bound to the man.

'All right,' she kept her voice as cool as possible, 'I'll let you have a coffee if you'll let me go.'

'A fair enough bargain,' he said, looking sardonic, and she felt his hand on her bare arm as he unbound her from the whip. Instantly she escaped into the *sala*, but just not quick enough to slam the doors in his face. With a lithe, silent swiftness he followed her into the room, and she knew from the mocking glint to his eyes that he had guessed her intention and was delighted that he had foiled it.

'I had better ring for a fresh cup and saucer,' she said, feeling the side of the silver pot and finding it still quite hot. She turned towards the bell-pull and he stepped in front of her, blocking the action that would bring a manservant to the *sala*.

'I don't mind drinking from your cup, Dina. I've drunk from muddy pools before now, so go ahead and pour for me—black, with one spoonful of sugar.'

She obeyed him, and felt unbearably conscious of him in this sunlit, chintzy room. He looked more foreign than ever, making her realise how people of the Latin races retained their look of the past, so that in fairly modern surroundings they seemed to step forward from a canvas which might have been painted by Titian or Tintoretto. Dina handed him the cup of coffee and as he slowly stirred in the sugar he glanced around the *sala*, taking in the circular writing-table and bookcase in amber walnut, the silky oak floor with its amethyst rugs, the lovely Romney painting above the ivory-coloured fireplace.

Sipping his coffee, he walked to the fireplace and gazed at the study of a young girl in a pale dress seated in a field of cornflowers, her fingers loosely entwined in the ribbons of her sash, her pale gold hair curling over her shoulder. The eyes in the portrait were enormous, and they were also of a golden colour.

'Lovely,' he murmured. '*Che bellezza!*'

He leaned a little forward to study the delicately portrayed face, and then he turned with almost military precision towards Dina. '*Intrigante,* would you not say? Painted by George Romney all those years ago, and yet it might be a portrait of you, Dina, when you were a child of fourteen.'

Dina flushed slightly under the piercing regard of his grey eyes. 'Bella, my godmother, bought it for that reason. She was in Europe at the time and came upon it at an auction; I believe it's a genuine Romney and not a copy by some clever artist.'

'It would certainly appear to be genuine. The eyes in the painting are very like yours, *signorina.* They have a candid gaze, and yet one wonders about the thoughts going on in that lovely head. At that age was your hair long?'

'Yes——' She tilted her chin. 'I prefer it bobbed for riding and swimming and being out on the golf course with Bay. Long fine hair becomes so untidy in the wind.'

'An attractive disarray,' he drawled. He lifted his coffee cup and drained it. 'You are still very young, so why should you mind if your hair gets tangled by the wind so that it resembles the mane of a Palomino filly? I have one of those, by the way, at my stables. She is being trained at present for next season's races—one day you must come over and ride her.'

'I don't think that would be very wise, Mr Ventura——'

'Discretion, wisdom, at your age?' He quirked a lip as he placed the empty cup and saucer on the silver tray. 'Those are virtues which should come with age, otherwise when you are in the autumn of your years you will look back and be sad that you didn't use your springtime as the birds and bees use it.'

Dina looked at him and couldn't help but notice how he brought into this room a vital aliveness. almost a flame which fascinated even as it aroused an active trepidation. He defied comparison to other men and challenged all that she kept in restraint deep within her. He would handle horses and women with daring and authority, and it was something she didn't dare to think about.

'You really are the devil in the garden, aren't you?' she said. 'Is the seduction of women your pastime?'

He gave a grating laugh and his eyebrows had a devilish slant to them as he moved about the room, examining its various *objets d'art*, picking them up with tapering dark fingers in order to feel the quality of the porcelain. He had the lithe movements of an animal. she thought, unselfconcious and also unpredictable.

'Why is it invariably assumed that men of Latin blood are more of a menace to the fair sex than men of the Northern races? It sometimes occurs to me that Cesare Borgia and Valentino did their compatriots no good at all, for we are now assumed to be untrustworthy and hot-blooded. The truth is, Miss Caslyn, that I often find more to admire in my racehorses than I find in females in general. A fine thoroughbred is sleek, silky, swift and beautifully tempered. Such a creature asks only for a stall of clean hay, a well-scrubbed carrot or an apple, a gallop in the fresh air, and some genuine affection.

Look what women demand of a man—his freedom, his unswerving attention, and most of his hard-earned money. And what does she give in return, eh? She either grows plump and sulky, or she takes to good works and becomes a seller of flags, tickets, and the left-off clothes of her friends.'

He picked up a pale ivory horse with its forelegs in the air, and he studied it with quizzical attention. 'My pastimes are my work, my horses, and the occasional fishing trip ... for barracuda.'

'It would be barracuda,' she murmured, and didn't believe for one minute that he didn't have a liking for women. It was there in his eyes, and in the way his lean hands caressed the antique ornaments, with a sensual enjoyment of the smooth contours. But they would be women that like these valuable pieces of bric-à-brac had some striking facet to their looks or personality. Raf Ventura might have worked his way up from dish-washer to entrepreneur, but on the way he had garnered more than a little knowledge about art and beauty.

He was a disturbing person, and she wished he would say *arrivederci* and ride off before Bella appeared.

Arrivederci! Her pulse jumped, for that was the Italian word for meeting again, not saying goodbye.

'I'm sure you have work to do, Mr Ventura,' she said, with an edge of desperation to the words. 'You hardly look the type to delegate any of your authority, having built your Sun Tower high and proud.'

'It does have a certain something, does it not?' He smiled, a brief glint of white teeth under that black moustache. 'My *torre paradisiaca*, with its white terraces and shining windows rising into the sun; with its scenic elevator climbing its walls like a glittering serpent. We have an Italian proverb which says that if you care greatly for something, then you should treat it with indifference in case the dark gods take notice.'

'Is that easy to do if you care for something?' she asked. 'And are you really so superstitious?'

'The Milanese are shrewd, but superstition stalks their blood like a grey cat in the shadows of an alley.' He shrugged his shoulders in a very Latin way. 'As to the other question—one learns to have the iron face, as we say.'

As he spoke his gaze was impossible to evade; the grey eyes had a steely quality that drew her glance to him against her will.

'Please go now,' she said, and it frightened her that she saw the iron in his face, and sensed in him those untamed forces from another land; the ruthless pleasure in his power to make her quail.

'Go!' She spoke the word sharply, almost like a cry of pain.

'Our vendetta isn't yet played out.' He flexed the whip in his hands, whose braided leather wasn't much darker than his skin. 'You do understand me, I presume?'

'You mean you're going to be vindictive because I——' There Dina broke off as she caught the sound of high heels on the oak floor beyond the hall door of the *sala*. She glanced wildly from the face of Raf Ventura to the door that was about to open.

'It's my godmother!'

If she had hoped that he would make a swift exit through the garden doors she was mistaken, for he stood there in his riding clothes, so sure of himself, so uncaring of how Bella would react to his presence, that Dina could have pushed him over ... had she possessed the muscle.

A middle-aged woman entered the room, made tall by the high-heeled shoes of crocodile skin that encased her narrow feet. She wore an expensively tailored silk suit, and every hair of her head was carefully in place and very precisely tinted to the chestnut it once had been. She had large features that now made her rather handsome, but in her youth, when she had been slimmer, she had not been considered a belle. It was said by those of her generation that she had attracted the wealthy Mark Rhinehart by her dominance, for he had been a man who had wanted his life run for him. Bella had succeeded very well in this, but a perceptive person might have seen deep in her dark brown eyes a residue of bitterness that she had not been the kind of girl to attract a dominant man.

Raf Ventura stood looking at her, his eyes as penetrating as actual steel. Dina felt as if she wanted to run off into the garden and not have to be part of the forthcoming duel between the two most dominating people she had ever met.

Bella Rhinehart returned his look and slowly raised an inquiring eyebrow. 'Have we met?' she asked, in her precise and cultured voice.

'In a manner of speaking,' he replied, and to Dina's ears his voice was as smooth and dangerous as ice over a dark gully.

The regal Bella swept her eyes up and down his tall, lean figure in the immaculate boots, breeches and hacking-jacket. 'Any visitors to this house are reported to me from the gate,' she said, and her eyes flashed to Dina, who flinched. 'Who is he?'

Bella demanded.

Forcing herself to speak calmly, Dina made the introduction. 'Mr Ventura and I met at the country club last week,' she added, and hoped to heaven that he wouldn't add that he had been there to discuss the buffet arrangements with the club secretary.

'Are you a new member, Mr Ventura?' Bella spoke his name in her most supercilious tone of voice, and Dina knew instantly that it would trigger him to a sardonic response.

'I've never subscribed to the select membership of clubs and Masonic orders,' he replied. 'I have business dealings with them and that is the extent of my interest.'

'Really?' There was a rustle of silk as Bella drew herself up haughtily. 'May I inquire your interest in coming here to my house without an invitation? It has always been understood between my goddaughter and myself that her acquaintances be made known to me so I can approve of them or not. A form of selectiveness which I subscribe to in the interest of Dina herself, for she has led a sheltered life and is less a judge of people——'

'Of men, do you mean?' he cut in.

'Yes, of men in particular. What business are you in, may I ask?' Once again Bella looked him up and down, and out of the corner of her eye Dina saw his hands grip and bend the handle of his whip.

'I run a hotel and restaurant, among other things, Mrs Rhinehart.'

Very audibly Bella caught her breath and the look she cast at Dina was sharp as acid.

He caught that look as well and his sardonic tone

of voice was even more pronounced as he added: 'You and Miss Caslyn stayed at my hotel several weeks ago, at Las Palmas, if you recall. I don't make it a rule that guests should be selected from a special list, but the idea has its appeal.'

Dina bit her lip, feeling the twitch of a humorous nerve. She had learned in her years with Bella never to have positive reactions about anything, for they were the prerogative of her godmother, but just now her reaction had been a treacherous desire to laugh, and Bella would have found that unforgivable. And deservedly so, for Bella had her best interest at heart ... whereas Raf Ventura had a far from saintly reason for coming here.

A glare of animosity came into Bella's eyes, for it wasn't often that anyone dared to be sarcastic at her expense. 'Did my goddaughter invite you into this house?' she demanded. 'Or have you had the audacity to push your way in?'

'I'm sure you know already, Mrs Rhinehart, that your goddaughter is too well trained to your slightest wish or whim to dare disobey you, so you may take it that I gatecrashed into your pleasance.' He glanced around him, until his gaze settled on the Romney portrait. 'A charming room, which would lose aspects of its charm without that painting above the fireplace. Would you part with it, I wonder?'

Bella's answer was to take a rapid step to the porcelain bell and give it an angry peal. 'A servant will show you out,' she said, in a brittle tone of voice. 'I don't think I need add that you are not invited to come again.'

'It is in my philosophy to believe that actions speak louder than words,' he drawled. 'The years don't mellow people as they do the trees and fine old houses, do they? Satanita has its attractions, especially as its iron bars aren't visible to the eye.'

With that lean, lithe precision of body he turned to Dina; he didn't speak right away and for a brief moment her eyes entreated him to go away and forget about her. If he saw what lay in her eyes he didn't transmit a reassurance that he would call off their vendetta.

He gave an inclination of his dark head. 'Perhaps we'll meet at Santa Luisa in the racing season. Don't be too shy to come and ask if I have any tips for a winner—I have an eye for a good runner.'

He sauntered towards the garden doors and there he gave Bella a parting salute with his whip shaft. He stepped outside, unloosened his mount's bridle from a tree and leapt with casual grace into the saddle. He rode off the way he had come, and Dina could feel the nervous beating of her heart as her godmother stood silently seething, having been denied the pleasure of having him shown out of Satanita by one of her servants.

'Why didn't you get Hudson and the dogs to run him off the place?' Bella turned and raked over Dina's face a look of anger and sharp curiosity. 'You haven't encouraged the man in any way, have you? His type are only too quick to take advantage of a lady, and I've made certain that you are one, Dina, and no Latin upstart is going to come here with his smart talk and his amorous ideas and undo all the work I've put into burying a scandal which could have ruined your life. If he approached you at the club dance, why did you say nothing to me about him?'

'I—I didn't think it important——'

'That isn't quite true, is it? Haven't we always been perfectly candid with each other? Haven't you always known that you're in a vulnerable position as my goddaughter and heiress—that man could be in the rackets from the look of him, and you should have told me at once that he'd had the temerity to approach you at the country club. Did you tell Bay—did he know?'

'Yes, he saw him, but I really dismissed him from my mind, Bella——'

'Then how come he turns up at Satanita, riding in here as if he's well acquainted with the place? He must have come in from the beach, and I really will have that pathway shut off with barbed wire——'

'Please, Bella, no.' Dina reached out and touched her godmother's arm, pleadingly. 'I'd feel a complete prisoner if I couldn't ride that way to the beach—I don't know how he found out about it, but he won't come again. He could see that he wasn't welcome.'

'Indeed not! It's obvious to me that the man has been watching you come and go, and I really feel that I should report the matter to Commissioner Fields—my God, we don't want a kidnapping!'

'Bella!' For a wild moment Dina didn't know whether to laugh or throw something, and there was temptation in the thought of hurling one of these carefully chosen *objets d'art* to the floor. Barbed wire, and no more dawn gallops with Major!

'Dear Bella, if the man was planning to kidnap me, he'd hardly come and show his face at Satanita. I expect he was trying to pick me up.'

Bella Rhinehart gave a visible shudder, and gave

instructions to the manservant at the door never to admit into the house a dark foreigner by the name of Ventura. 'And bring some fresh coffee.' She indicated the tray. 'And *croquants*.'

'Yes, madam.' He lifted the tray, slid his eyes across Dina's face, and went quietly from the *sala*.

'Now there'll be gossip in the kitchen.' Bella paraded back and forth across the room, and her striking face had assumed its tragic look. Dina was never sure if tragedy was a genuine feeling in Bella, who always seemed so in command of her own life and other people's. She had known tragedy, of course, some years before Dina had been brought to Satanita to live. She and her husband had been on a trip to the Alps and he had plunged down a mountainside on his skis, straight into a raging cascade of icy water. Bella hadn't married again, but it often struck Dina that she must have come to care for Lewis Caslyn, otherwise why would she have taken on the sole care of his only child?

'*Dushechka,*' in this mood Bella was inclined to become rather Tolstoy, 'darling soul child, I've only ever wanted the best for you, and that is not a Latin gambler who runs a restaurant.' She half-closed her heavy white eyelids. 'You are my ward of court, Judge Manders made it so, and if this man tries hanging around you, then I'll see to it that he goes to jail. I have that kind of influence, and you know it, don't you?'

'Yes, Bella.' For an instant Dina felt stricken and she sat down on the chintz divan nearest to the french windows and felt the garden scents waft across her skin. 'But you're exaggerating the entire episode, I do assure you. Because he happens to be

63

Italian that doesn't mean that he's some kind of a Mafia ringleader.'

'No one ever knows. No one can ever be sure.' Bella flung out her hands in a dramatic movement so her rings flashed. 'But he's a gambler right enough, you heard him mention the Santa Luisa race track, and his knack for picking a good runner. Dina, how dare you even speak to such a man? Haven't I taught you how to behave with people who aren't our sort?'

'Yes, I'm supposed to give them the cold shoulder.'

'Exactly so.' Bella paused by the long windows with an air of injured majesty. 'I hope I haven't to face the awful prospect that you might let me down, not after all I've done for you, and the way I've cared for you. I have cared, Dina. You've been the child I never had, and it has made me proud that you've grown up so fair and lovely. That's it, of course! A man sees beauty and he either stumbles over his own feet, or he reaches out with greedy hands. This Ventura has reached out, and I'll see him in court, consigned to a cell, before you are touched by his hands!'

Dina's own hands clenched the chintz covering of the divan. 'Please don't say such things,' she pleaded. 'They aren't called for.'

'Aren't they?' Bella moved and came over to Dina, standing above her with eyes like brown stones. 'You know how your father got into trouble, don't you? You aren't innocent of the fact that he became involved with such men—well, I won't stand for it a second time, do you hear me? Lewis, the fool, was ruined by such an association, and I won't allow anything like that to happen to you. I forbid you to see this man ever again, and if he should ever dare approach you, then you are to tell me and I'll have him stopped.'

Bella leaned down and took Dina by the chin, holding her and looking deep into her eyes. 'Do I make myself clear, Dina?'

'Yes.' A shiver went through Dina and she felt as if ice had collected in the pit of her stomach. Bella Rhinehart had great wealth and friends in high places, and there seemed little doubt that she could cause trouble for anyone who threatened the orderly pattern of the life she had mapped out for her protégée. She had spent time, money and attention on the child whom Lewis Caslyn had consigned to the devil, and Dina's gratitude was shadowed by the feeling that she had lost her freedom and was, as Raf Ventura had said, the prisoner of a castle whose iron bars weren't visible to the eye.

But her heart felt them ... her heart was surely locked inside those bars of iron.

Bella gripped her by the chin, the point of her thumb in the delicate cleft at its base. 'You will not see this—this hotel-keeper ever again.' The words ripped into Dina. 'I'll have your promise, or you'll be confined to this house, to your very room.'

'I didn't ask him to come here,' Dina said indignantly. 'Why should I be treated like a capricious child?'

'You must have given him some sign—some indication of interest.'

'But I didn't!'

'Men pick up signals, and girls aren't always aware of making them.'

'Bella, I've never made signals to any man—even Bay. I'm not a flirt and you know it!'

'I knew your father, remember, and instincts in the blood are stronger than we realise. You know what his life came to—the sheer waste of it in gambling and speculation, and then living in a cloud of white wine until he ended it all. He cared for you despite his behaviour, but he was weak, Dina, and I don't want to see you following in his footsteps. I'll take severe measures to prevent it.'

'Have I ever let you down?' Dina asked quietly. 'Have I ever been less than grateful for the life you've given me? I know how wild and irresponsible my father was, and how I'd have grown up had he kept me with him——'

Dina paused and couldn't prevent a deep sigh. 'All the same, he might not have taken that final step, had I been there with him.'

'You think not?' Bella frowned and stood there with the sunlight behind her, so that her features looked dark, and her eyes even darker. 'I think he died because he was afraid to go on living. My lawyer had prevented him from going to prison, but there were men who had—I think the Italians have a word for it—a vendetta against Lewis Caslyn.'

Dina stared at her godmother with shocked eyes —that word again, which Raf Ventura had used. That implication of sweet revenge, the day of reckoning, Nemesis.

In that silence filled with heartbeat the *sala* door opened and a maid in frilled apron and trim lace cap carried in a tray of fresh coffee and the crisp biscuits Bella liked, straight from the oven and folded into a white napkin on one of the Chinese porcelain plates. The maid lowered the tray to the divan table, and once again Dina felt the brief flick

66

of inquisitive eyes. It was a rare thing for Bella and herself to argue, and the staff would be aware that a dark masculine stranger had appeared at the house and they would guess that he was the apple of discord being tossed back and forth in the *sala*, usually a room of sunlit harmony underscored by the crackle of biscuit and the pages of the morning papers being turned.

'That will be all, Lilian.' Bella came to the divan. 'I'll pour the coffee myself—oh, and tell Norwich that I shall want the car at the steps by ten-thirty. I have to go into town.'

'Yes, madam.' The maid carefully closed the door behind her, and the strained atmosphere in the *sala* was increased for Dina by her godmother's remark about needing the car. Bella usually spent an hour in the orchid house before setting off for her appointments in town, and there seemed a hint of threat in her announcement.

'Will you take a cup?' Bella asked, pouring the hot and aromatic brew from the imp-chased pot which Dina had used earlier on, pouring coffee for Raf Ventura into her own cup. A man who had washed dishes in the hot kitchens of restaurants, who had drunk from muddy pools out on the battlefields, and who had come here bringing with him the dark whisper of vendetta.

'No, thanks, I've had mine.' Dina sat there, her spine tensed against the soft cushions. 'May I ride into town with you, Bella? I want to see if my new riding-boots are ready; they have to be broken in for the hunt next Thursday.'

Bella lifted her cup and studied Dina's face over the rim. She sipped in silence for a moment or two, then she said: 'Yes, I am going into town to see

Ralph Quinton, if you're curious, Dina. I'm going to ask him to make inquiries about this Ventura person, and if there is anything at all shady about the man, which Ralph can actually use, then I'm going to have him stopped from ever daring to speak to you again. I have nurtured you and brought you to the very threshold of a brilliant marriage with one of the most eligible young men of this county, and I won't have my plans threatened in any way at all. Do you take me for a fool, Dina? Don't you think I know that you aren't head over heels in love with Bay? But what is love? Love! It is more like falling headlong into the jaws of a tiger shark. It can tear you to pieces, scatter your heart from your head, and it just isn't worth that moonlit swim in the seas of rapture that end in torment. Take it from me!'

Bella had never spoken like this before, and it also shook Dina that she had guessed that it was only fondness and respect that she felt for Bay Bigelow. Bella wanted it that way, for she obviously didn't believe that a passionate love brought happiness with it.

'I wouldn't deliberately do anything to hurt Bay or you, Bella.' Dina spoke with a quiet intensity, without a hint of the rebellion that might stir deep in her soul, putting out the tiny quills that brought pain and the awareness of what it might feel like to be totally alive to a man. In place of all that she had security and she couldn't risk it.

'Please, Bella, don't for goodness' sake go and see Mr Quinton. There is no need, and there is the danger—you spoke just now about tiger sharks. Some men are like that. Dare to prod them, or to question their integral strength, and they'll turn on you. Don't do it, Bella! I beg of you!'

Dina had never felt so sure of anything, that if challenged Raf Ventura would turn very dangerous. It had been apparent in his lean command of his body, in his eyes whose metallic grey was like the armour of a gliding shark. He would come close and let her feel the abrasion of his touch, but he wouldn't snap those dangerous teeth and spill her blood ... unless someone forced him to take a defensive action.

'Let's forget him,' Dina pleaded. 'Why make such an issue of the man? As you said yourself, Bella, his type are predatory and best avoided.'

Bella took a biscuit and carried it to her lips. 'Then he frightened you?' she said.

'Not exactly.' Dina shook her head, silvery-fair in the sunlight streaming into the room. Around the expanded pupils of her eyes the amber irises were like rings of gold. 'I was furious that he should dare to use my special rideway, and I don't wish to see his arrogant face ever again. He knows, Bella, how I feel about him.'

Biscuit crunched, the Limoges clock ticked, and Dina silently prayed that Bella would abandon her plan to go and see her lawyer and maybe set in motion what Dina feared ... a real vendetta that Raf Ventura would pursue with all the relentlessness of which he was capable. No man worked and thrived as he had done without having a relentless nature, and she knew her own sensitive recoil from inflicting hurt on anyone. She would ride with the hunt next week and only the gallop across country would give her any pleasure. The chase itself would be hateful to her, and all the time she would be praying that the hounds didn't pick up the scent of a vixen, or the fire-red fox with its bushy tail.

Sitting here she had rather a trapped feeling, and could recall vividly her reaction to Bay when he had once presented her with the brush after a successful chase ... she had swung Major away from the laughing crowd in their bright coats and deliberately jibbed him. The horse had dashed off with her and the action had looked genuine enough for Bay to ride after her, bent on rescue. He hadn't guessed to this day that Dina had been repelled by the snapping, clawing hounds, and the terrified inability of the fox to escape them. That was the only time she had really disliked him, and she had sense enough to realise that he wasn't cruel at heart, but had seen and done things in Vietnam that made a fox hunt no more to him than swiping a summer fly that buzzed around a ham sandwich he might be eating.

This dark Italian was something else. *Il tigre*, she thought, a man who could be truly ruthless ... primitive and unrestrained if driven to it. His desires would be arrogant, and his heart would not be easily moved, and Dina had to control the urge to actually beg her godmother not to use her influence to make some kind of charge against him, that of housebreaking, or even attempted seduction of her ward. Dina didn't doubt that he'd be clever enough to disprove the charges, and then having disproved them he'd set out to have his own back on *her*.

She'd be his victim because she was already vulnerable as the child of Lewis Caslyn. Like turtle eggs, no scandal could be buried deep enough from the tearing claws, and Bella must have seen what lurked in Dina's eyes, a terror of fresh scandal that might reawaken whispers of the past, for she said grudgingly:

'Very well, I'll not consult Ralph Quinton upon this occasion, but the warning is there, Dina. I want this marriage between you and Bay to take place; it will be advantageous in several respects, and it will set the final seal on your acceptance into society. You're an unusually attractive girl, and in a few more years you'll be one of Pasadena's most stunning young women, and you could influence Bay into following Senator Bigelow into politics. Who knows? In our democracy anything is possible, and what wouldn't I have given to have attracted a man with a political background.'

Dina heard all this without fully taking it in ... her main feeling was one of deep relief that Bella had called off her 'hounds' and wasn't going to start a tiger chase.

She broke into a smile, but in the palms of her hands were beads of perspiration, and her spine felt as if it would crack from the tension she had endured since that moment she had glanced up from her newspaper and seen Raf Ventura ride into the garden court.

She hoped to heaven that she wouldn't see again that proud, hard, passionate face, that raven hair with a metallic sheen at the temples, those Cagliostro eyes with their magnetism, their irony, and their steely grey shield that concealed his secrets.

'As Norwich will be bringing round the car, you might as well use it to go and see about your riding-boots,' Bella said. 'I'm pleased you hunt, Dina. The apparel suits you, for you've the right type of figure. The overly lush female never looks good in breeches and boots, let alone a well-tailored riding-coat.'

Bella poured another cup of coffee, and she studied Dina from head to heel, as if checking over the points which had made her worth cultivating in the first place. The fey cheekbones tapering to a triangular jaw, the wide expressive mouth and fine eyebrows shading eyes amber and faintly slanting.

'Petite cat,' Bella murmured. 'You aren't like me, are you? You suffer a lot of terrors I never felt, and in a way I envy your sensitive nature and yet feel grateful that I'm harder and bolder. The world is a jungle, and Bay will be a dependable keeper. So be careful, don't start feeling an urge to explore, there's a good child.'

Dina felt as if she had been patted on the head by a firm but basically kind hand. She felt instinctively that some return was due, and she rose and bent over Bella and gently kissed her cheek.

'Thank you,' she murmured.

'For what exactly?' Bella gazed up at Dina and a hint of curiosity moved in her eyes.

'Oh, for being so good to me. Not everyone would have taken such care of a child from a—a criminal background.'

'Lewis wasn't a criminal, he was a fool with too much charm and not enough backbone when it came to facing up to those who led him into games he wasn't tough enough to play. Forget him, Dina. Don't look over your shoulder, but look ahead to the day when you wear white silk and make the society pages as the bride of the year. Time is getting on. We must soon think about choosing the material and having the first fittings for your dress. Something that will go perfectly with diamonds, for they're your stone and Mamie Bigelow has already hinted that Bay will be buying the Tyler-Brandon stones that are coming up for sale at Tiffanys.'

Bella drew a deep, satisfied sigh. '*Pussinka moiya*, you will shine on that day. Doesn't the thought of it make your heart flutter?'

'Yes,' Dina could say, truthfully.

It fluttered with a kind of inevitable terror, for the white silk and diamonds were symbols of a love she didn't truly feel, and wanted with a kind of desperation to feel. Security would then be bliss if only she could curl into Bay's arms and give him her soul as well as her slim body.

Oh, she would never cheat him, she was convinced of that ... but supposing, just supposing she glanced across a room and looked into a pair of eyes that beckoned her into that jungle which Bella had mentioned. That hot and menacing jungle of the emotions, where strange whispers and enticing shadows could lead a woman so easily astray.

'I'm off. 'Bye for now, Bella!'

Dina hastened from the *sala*, and from thoughts that kept whispering that she had glanced across a room and looked into the eyes of *il tigre*, the most sinister and fascinating occupant of any jungle.

She snatched a coat from the hall cupboard and went out to the gleaming car with its sun roof open. 'I'm using the car in place of Mrs Rhinehart,' she told the chauffeur. 'Drive at a good pace, Norwich. I want to feel the wind in my mind.'

A Freudian slip she was entirely aware of.

The chauffeur, smart in his brown uniform smiled as he opened the passenger door and Dina sank down against the beige velour of the upholstery. Most of the staff had known her from a child and they treated her as the daughter of the house, with never a hint that it was otherwise. Dina was aware of their liking for her, and their loyalty; what she was unaware of was that her own youthful dignity and kindness made it easy for them to be kind and considerate in return.

'A lovely autumn morning, Miss Dina,' said Norwich. 'Shall I take the coast road into town?'

'Mmmm, please. This is my favourite season of the year, and I almost wish that time could stand still.'

'Only it never does, Miss Dina. It's like the tides, and as certain as the stars—they'll shine come rain or tears; peace or war.'

Norwich took his place behind the wheel and they drove past the pomegranate walk, with its rusty gold fruit and its dappled fountain, leading into the heart of the estate where the jays had their hiding-places, and the red squirrels and some small deer were like vagrants from Disneyland.

Dina knew what love of a house felt like; and she had a warm regard and affection for the woman who had shared Satanita with her ... but born in her soul on this autumn day was a curiosity about that strange and shattering force that sometimes bound a woman to a man.

That she should feel curious was an indication, had she needed one, that what she felt for her future husband was serenely devoid of passion. An *affaire aimable*, with the feelings as undisturbed as one of the garden pools where the waterlilies floated on their own green islands.

Trust me all in all, or trust me not at all. Was that the meaning of love, that you dived in blindly,

74

trusting against the darkest odds, risking body and soul in the ecstasy of that plunge into deep, deep waters?

The wheels of the car sang on the wide stretch of coastal road, and there on one side were the sweeping chaparral hills patched with autumn gold and flame, and far below on the left was the ocean, burning like steel in the sun, the unfathomable depths falling away beneath that shimmering surface.

Dina sat silent, staring beyond the window, and knew herself in the grip of a fear that was also strangely exciting. Looking down into the ocean was like being drawn into silvery-grey eyes that beckoned and held subtle glints of laughter ... smiling as the devil himself might smile.

'Oh no,' she cried out, silently. 'Let go of my thoughts ... let go of *me*!'

CHAPTER THREE

HORSES, riders and hounds streamed across country like a colourful hunting print which had come magically to life. Dina Caslyn was at the rear of the chase, deliberately holding back her powerful grey Major, determined not to be at the fore if the hounds should suddenly scent a fox.

The hooves of the other horses pounded ahead of her, and her hand was firm on the reins of her horse, a natural born hunter with a competitive streak in him, who could have outdistanced most of the animals in the field and yet was too much of a thoroughbred to disobey any whim of the girl in his saddle. He had been hers from a foal, having been born on a night of storm when Dina was sixteen and home from school for the summer vacation. She had woken to the sounds of distress from the stables at the rear of Satanita and had hurried down in her pyjamas and hastily thrown-on raincoat, arriving in time to see the vet lifting the foal from the dead body of its mother. From that moment Major had been hers to care for, to rear and train, and a deep bond of understanding existed between them.

Major was one of the few reasons why she hunted, for he loved the thrill of the chase, and she would let him out into a full gallop as soon as they fell far enough behind the pack to be able to ride off at a tangent. Later on she would pretend that she hadn't noticed she was heading in the wrong direction; no one would really mind, for Dina was accepted as a rather private sort of person, in some ways a bit of a dreamer but lovely enough to be forgiven most things. Besides, she belonged to Bay and he was the *homme idéal* of the charmed circle, and his girl was naturally *sans peur et sans reproche*.

The sun slanted in a gale of gold across the fields, the pounding of hooves had a rhythm of their own, constant as a distant drummer. A hint of dusky flame was burning among the trees, which made spires where dark birds had their hauntings.

The moment had come for Dina to break free of the hunt, and with a sudden smile she did so, turning Major in the other direction and allowing him to release his muscles in a long, loping stride. A quick thrill of relief blazed in her eyes, setting them alight beneath the brim of a jaunty suede hat, worn with a checked riding coat, suede waistcoat underneath, and pale beige breeches tucked into suede boots to the knee. Most members of the club wore the traditional hunting clothes, but Dina had put her boot firmly down on the notion of wearing the garb that proclaimed one a lover of a blood sport, and the further away she rode from the clamour of the hounds—a shrill note in their baying, as if quarry had been scented at last—the happier she felt.

She knew that Bay would be riding alongside the master of the hounds, and that he would have forgotten for the time being that she was taking part in the chase—or supposed to be taking part. Later on he would ask her casually if she had enjoyed herself, and if, as now, she had managed to break free and ride alone she would be able to reply with truth that she had loved the gallop.

Bay was an extrovert who rarely delved into her private thoughts; he admired her looks and liked her cool composure, and like many other young men of his class he didn't wish to associate passionate loves or hates with the woman he took as his wife. He didn't dream how passionate was Dina's dislike of the cruelty that ended a chase. He hadn't the remotest idea that her coolness was like the icing on a *bombe* of tangy fruit baked in hot brandy.

Dina didn't fully know herself ... except that she was Lewis Caslyn's daughter, and he had been no angel!

There was silence except for Major's rhythmic hoofbeats, and then across that silence echoed the sound of a hunting horn, and the nerves of her heart tightened. 'Go!' she cried at Major, and he bounded into a full gallop, taking a rise that dipped into a hollow, darkening into a tunnel of tall trees. It made a sounding chamber for the pounding of his hooves, and it closed out whatever shrill echoes might have come from over the hills, where she sensed that a fox had been trapped and was probably being torn to pieces at this very moment. Anger and pity so blinded her eyes that she didn't notice that a barred gate of some height lay ahead of her galloping mount. When he braced his muscles and jumped it, Dina was unprepared for the sudden leap, though instinctively she kicked free of the stirrups as she felt herself being ejected from the saddle. As it happened there were plenty of leaves in the woods, which had fallen into piles, and she landed not too badly, stunning her right elbow in the fall, but even so she was anxious that Major wouldn't dash off and leave her stranded. She gave the whistle which should have signalled him to a halt, but something seemed to have spooked him and he went cantering off among the trees, dragging his reins and leaving Dina to scramble to her feet, her left hand cradling her stinging elbow.

'Major!' She whistled him again, but he refused to respond, and annoyed with herself for taking a tumble which was entirely her own fault, she said, 'Damn!' and stamped a booted foot.

'Temper, temper,' drawled a voice, and she swung round on the instant and found herself confronting the man she had so fervently hoped she would never see again.

'You!' she exclaimed.

'I, *signorina*.' He gave her a sardonic bow and swept his eyes up and down her dishevelled figure.

Already shaken and in a temper, Dina was in no mood just then to choose her words. 'You've been following me,' she accused. 'Making quarry of me like—like those hounds after a vixen!'

'Have I now?' His left eyebrow slanted, and the play of lacy sunlight on the strong dark angles of his face made him more sinister in this moment than she had yet seen him.

'You didn't wave your sorcerer's wand, Don Mephisto,' she said cuttingly. 'Magic belongs in children's story books, so the conclusion is that you've been tracking me down!'

'Are you really so certain that you don't believe in magic?' His smile was subtle, there in the darting gleams of gold and shadow. 'I knew the hunt was out, but I thought you'd be in the thick of it with your fiancé, eager for the kill.'

'I hate the kill!' She angrily brushed leaves and twigs from her breeches, and then tautened in every nerve as she felt his hand brushing her jacket. 'Don't do that—I can manage!'

'I had the impression that your elbow took a nasty whack.'

'It's only a bruise. I've tumbled out of the saddle before and lived to ride again.' She stepped away from his proximity and flung back her head with that instinctive air of pride and independence, and a shading of the fear she couldn't quite banish from her eyes. A ray of sunlight tangled itself in her hair, from which her suede hat had fallen, and the cleft in her chin was so beautifully marked as to seem almost a shadow in her fine bone-structure.

'So you hate to see the fear-crazed vixen being torn by the hounds and watched by the intrepid hunters, waiting to take their trophy in the shape of the poor brute's tail. How the high and mighty find their pleasures!'

'How do you find yours?' she shot at him. 'In hunting women? Are they your prey, *signore*?'

'At least it's a more humane sport, for the woman is permitted to run away when the game is over.'

'Oh, don't you take their scalps and hang them on your bedpost?' The words were out before Dina could stop them, and the hand she flung upwards couldn't push them back in her mouth.

'So you are human and not made from beautifully chiselled ice.' He gave a laugh and lounged against the trunk of a tree, clad in a brown shirt and matching trousers, a light-coloured jacket cloaking his shoulders. 'Are you aware, by the way, that you and your horse are trespassing on private land?'

'Nonsense,' she said at once. 'These woods are part of the old Penrose estate, which has been empty and abandoned since Adam Penrose died a dozen years ago. He and his wife lived a rather odd sort of life and some people said she was—mad, that's why the house has been difficult to sell. Bella reckons it will eventually be pulled down and the land parcelled off to a speculator.'

'Bella Rhinehart is a shrewd woman, but upon this occasion she has fired and missed the bullseye,' he drawled. 'Adam's Challenge has been sold and will once again be occupied, when the necessary repairs and adjustments have been made by the new owner.'

Dina gazed at him in sheer amazement. 'You have to be kidding,' she said. 'The place has gone to seed and it would take a man of quite some means to put it back in shape. Only a speculator would bother with such a property, surely?'

When he just stood there looking at her, sliding a hand into his pocket for his cheroot case, a premonition touched her and warned her that she was facing the new owner of that brooding Colonial mansion, white-stoned and proud half a century ago, but now a lonely and sombre hulk with its windows shuttered to keep out vagrants. It had a large rectangular courtyard, curving bays, and stood on a knoll overgrown with weeds and vine-strangled shrubs. Few people went near the place after dark, for the Penrose couple had been strange and solitary people. He had been a folk-lorist, who tramped the countryside in a wide-brimmed hat and a great cloak, like some character from a

81

Victorian gothic novel, and his wife had kept to her rambling garden, singing to herself in a language no one had fully understood. The sound of her tuneless incantations floating over the garden walls had led to the belief that she was crazy ... all that was really known *was that* after she died Adam Penrose became even more morose and in a few short years followed her, leaving no heirs or known relatives, and the old house known as Adam's Challenge had fallen into decay, no one being resolute enough to live there and recharge the property with new life.

Raf Ventura clicked shut his lighter and blue smoke clouded about his face and streamed off into the red-gold rays of afternoon sunshine, prodding their way through the boughs of the trees.

'Would not an entrepreneur have the audacity to do it?' he drawled.

'Yes, I suppose so,' she admitted, and she hardly dared to face the fact that he meant to live at Adam's Challenge; to make of it his home ... which would then be only a few short miles from Satanita. 'Are you going to have it bulldozed and rebuilt into an estate of bungalows, Mr Ventura?'

'You would like to think so, wouldn't you, Miss Caslyn?' The wreathing smoke intensified his sardonic look, playing about his steely grey eyes under the slanting black brows. 'I wonder what turn the gossip will take when the matriarchs of Pasadena learn that an Italian *restaurateur* is going to make his home among them? Will they try and have me run out, do you think, and will your godmother lead the chase?'

He hit very close to a nerve and recalled vividly for Dina the way she had pleaded with Bella not to make an enemy of this man by getting her lawyer to probe into his private life. If he had purchased the house, then Bella would ultimately learn of it and Dina knew she would be powerless to prevent her godmother from hounding him. Why did Bella feel driven to do so? Because years ago Lewis had got himself disastrously involved with a gambling syndicate of this man's nationality? Or because she saw in him a threat to Dina and the forthcoming marriage she had so skilfully encouraged?

Dina bent down to retrieve her hat and because her nerves were shaken she gave it an extra hard thump against the side of her breeches in order to remove the leaf dust. 'I must catch hold of Major if I can ... may I go and find him? He'll have ventured right into the grounds of the house by now.'

'We'll go together,' he said at once. 'You might even permit me to show you around my newly acquired property.'

'I—I don't think I shall have the time——'

'You're over eighteen, aren't you, and not completely shackled to the godmother. You might like the house—some of its rooms are beautifully proportioned, and the place might take on quite an air once I've licked it into shape. I'm going to, Dina. I've been looking for a suitable home for a long time, and this is it, and I don't care a sizzle in hell what Bella Rhinehart and her coterie say, or attempt to do. I plan to make Adam's Challenge my home, whenever I can snatch the time from my business concerns to enjoy the novelty of being a householder.'

'Oh, so you won't be here all the time?' Try as she might Dina couldn't keep the note of relief out of her voice, and he gave a sudden, rather hard laugh that startled some birds in the trees overhead; there was a flutter of wings as they flew out from their perch, circling restlessly, as if, Dina thought, a tiger had prowled into their forest.

'I can't quite make out if you genuinely dislike me,' he said, 'or find me a trifle too intriguing for comfort.'

'You've a dollar on yourself,' she rejoined. 'Why should I find you even a trifle intriguing?'

'Because I'm different from your set, Dina, and come from another world. Because I've washed dishes in restaurant kitchens hot and seething as the back premises of hell itself. Because I got born as near dark as the devil without actually having the cloven hoofs.'

'You might have those, for all I know.' Their combined footsteps fell together on the leaf-strewn pathway, and she glanced as she spoke at the hand-tailored gleam of his mahogany-toned shoes. He had long and narrow feet, and he walked with the noiseless grace of the Latin. She was intrigued by him, and there was no denying it. He was different from the people she had grown up with ... from those athletic boys who wouldn't know how to put dishes in a sink without splashing themselves with greasy water from neck to knee.

It was incredible that this well-shod, darkly groomed, subtly intelligent man had ever washed and stacked dishes; served food and smiled upon the diners in that abstractedly polite way of waiters. To say she was intrigued was to put it too tamely. The awareness evoked by his vital, restless, untamed personality made her want to dash away into the heart of the woods and escape his sorcery.

Yes, he was casting a spell which she was afraid of, for there was a dark excitement to it that was leading her, even at this moment, into the house of strange secrets which he had bought for himself. Why had he bought the place? To infuriate people like Bella? To compensate for youthful poverty? Or to be close enough to Satanita to come upon herself as he had this afternoon?

As the shadows of the woods lifted and they came out by a side gate that had fallen brokenly to one side, Dina caught the jingle of a bridle and knew that Major was nearby. She hurried forward, calling his name, and found him fetlock-deep in a patch of tall grass, filling his belly with the lush green stuff.

'There you are, you bad old boy!' Dina ran to him and caught hold of his reins. Raf Ventura strolled forward and stood there giving the horse a thorough scrutiny.

'Good blood, eh, and quite a bit of speed in those sleek muscles. You must be a very capable rider to be able to manage him, Dina.'

'I've been riding since I was a child,' she said, stroking a hand down Major's long glossy neck. 'He can go at quite a lick, can't you, my handsome grey?'

'You'll have to challenge me to race, when I've got things straightened out and can stable a horse or two at Adam's Challenge.' The grey eyes swept over Dina as she stood there beside her mount, very slender in her riding clothes. 'It crosses my mind that with your cap of flaxen hair you look rather like a Renaissance pageboy,' he added lazily.

'I'd prefer it, *signore*, if you didn't say things like that.' Her pulses had quickened and she was strongly tempted to leap into Major's saddle and be off like the wind, and as if he sensed this impulse in her body he came across and took hold of the horse's reins and latched them around a nearby tree.

'Would it be different if I were part of the local *beau monde*?' he drawled, lifting lean fingers and letting Major nuzzle them. Dina stared, for it was unusual for the proud grey to accept so readily the caress of a stranger.

'What do you mean—different?'

'Acceptable. Able to pay you a compliment without putting you into a panic.'

'I'm not in a panic,' she denied. 'Why should I be?'

'Because we're alone, Dina. Because we're a man and a woman—oh, to hell with the diamonds on your hand, if you're about to throw in my face that you are all too soon to be a married lady.'

'It's true, all the same.' For the life of her she couldn't stop her voice from shaking a little. 'I—I don't mind being friends, if you want that?'

'Ah, what a concession from the princess!'

'Please—just be friends.'

'We don't appear to be enemies, Dina.'

'I'd hate that, to be enemies with you——' She broke off sharply and could have bitten her tongue for such an admission.

'What a confession,' the edge of his moustache lifted in that ironic smile of his, 'and drawn from you without the aid of rack or fire.'

'Don't!' She shivered in the shards of sunlight falling down from the treetops. 'There's something curiously medieval about you, *signore*.'

'Shades of Cesare Borgia and Cagliostro, eh?'

'Oh yes—you are in some ways a sorcerer, aren't you?'

'From dishes to riches, do you mean, in the course of twenty years?'

'Yes—you let nothing stand in your way. You meant to be part of—of my world, and so you bought this place.' She swung round and gestured at the house, so long neglected, so possibly haunted, with sheets of lichen clinging to its side walls, its steps meshed in cat's foot ivy, great hands of fern, and ribbon grass gone wild, twining around the elder trees like petrified witches.

And yet ... Dina was too sensitive, too imaginative not to see that despite its neglect and its decadence Adam's Challenge had a strange sort of charm.

The roof tiles sloped at an angle, they curved in almost a poetic way and were rusty red. Gabled windows were set high and deep in the roof, where long attics were situated. Below ran a carved stone frieze with heraldic designs, to which at intervals the pillars of the great porch were attached. Set in the porch itself was a fine oriole window, like Penelope's web, and the colonnade stretched to left and right, curving into great bays. Behind the house rose the wooded hills, so close they seemed part of it, as if the place grew out of them. It was impossible to deny the worn beauty and weathered charm that still clung to the house which Raf Ventura had decided to own.

'No,' he shook his head at her, 'I have no desire to be part of your world, but come with me and be part of mine for just a while.'

'I really should be getting home——' And yet she was curious to see inside, and it seemed as if a look almost wistful touched the lean Italian face that turned to her.

'Go, then.' He wasn't going to persuade her, or force her to enter the house with him. He mounted the front steps and took from his coat pocket a bunch of keys, but he didn't unlock the door right away. By the side of it, attached to the wall, was an old-fashioned horn, such as might have been seen in the porchways of old English castles, and taking it by the chain he blew on it and at the hollow, booming sound Dina expected all the hounds of hell to come running.

Unexpectedly she laughed and followed him up the steps. 'All right, I'm sold on a sightseeing tour, Mr Ventura. You've piqued my curiosity, but I can't stay long—will you have the name changed? The challenge part is fine for you, but not the Adam, somehow.'

'Not foreign enough, eh?' He glanced into her eyes with a look of amused irony. 'I daresay my house will soon be christened the Villa Mafioso by the local bucks.'

'I—I didn't mean anything like that,' she flushed slightly. 'I meant that Adam is rather tame for you—you'd never let anyone make a fool of you, least of all a woman.'

'Man was made to be tempted, Dina, otherwise that little drama wouldn't have taken place in Eden.' As he spoke he swung open the pair of tall doors opening into the hall, and there on the threshold Dina hesitated, feeling compelled, yet feeling as if fate were at her heels.

'Will you be living here alone, or have you a——?'

'I'm unmarried.' He closed the doors as she followed him inside and the gloom and dust of the place settled around them. 'But were you wondering if I had an *inamorata*?'

'I was betting on it,' she retorted.

'That I'd bring a mistress to Adam's Challenge and really set the matrons on fire with indignation?' He gave a short, hard laugh and strode across to a large oak sideboard which had been partly uncovered from a dusty sheet. Candles stood there in tarnished holders and he lit them with his lighter, moving it back and forth across the wicks until they smoked and burst into flame. One of them burned with almost a blue flame and Dina stared at it, and then glanced around the hall, which towered upwards past the galleries until there was nothing but shadow.

'Take one of these, for the shutters are still up in most of the rooms.' The play of the candle flames deepened the crevices in his face and his deep-throated voice fluttered the bright smoking tongues as he handed her one of the holders. She took it and followed him across the hall into a large, bow-fronted room.

'I plan to use this as my dining-room, and the one that matches it as the living-room.' He held aloft his candlestick and played the fluttering light over walls hung with faded olive-green velvet; a large room with a gloom of its own, whose secrets were locked in its cupboards and lost in the folds of faded brocade at the windows. Each creak of a floorboard seemed to betray the presence of a ghost, and as Dina stepped on to the carpet, spotted with moth-holes and heavy with dust, she gave a sudden sneeze.

'Bless your mother,' he murmured. 'As they say

in Italy.'

Dina refused to look at him and gazed instead at the Chippendale table which had been uncovered from its dust sheet, nicked and scratched, and obviously vandalised by a writer who had also carved his own woodcuts.

'Oh, what a pity,' she said. 'It looks genuine, and Adam Penrose has treated it like a schoolboy's desk.'

'Most of the furniture is excellent, but it hasn't been cared for,' he agreed. 'That sideboard against the wall is also antique, but at some time or other a candle has fallen over and burned the wood. Can't you imagine a cluster of silver chafing dishes on it?'

'Muffins, kippers, and farmhouse eggs,' she murmured.

'The other room is even more evocative. Come and see, Dina.'

She followed him through the double doors into the adjoining room, where the chairs and sofas were robed in grimy white sheets and turned into ghost furniture. Here there was a strangely haunting smell, like the scent of damp violets, and the long mirrors had been turned to the wall.

'Who would have done that?' Dina all but whispered.

'Someone who had reason to fear storms,' he replied. 'The Penrose couple were not American, you know. I was told they came originally from Cornwall, which I understand is the land's end of the British Isles. Something tragic happened to their daughter and it sent the woman quietly but harmlessly crazy. Come, I think I found the daughter when I came here the other day, in one of the upstairs rooms.'

Like a pair of conspirators they made their way

to the staircase which curved away into the gloom of the galleries, with a fine blackwood balustrade that would gleam like ebony when it was finally cleaned and polished. Raf Ventura mounted that sweep of stairs with the grace and control of a jungle cat, but Dina could feel the faint quiver in her legs at knowing herself so alone with him in this big dark house, with a belt of trees all around to render it strangely quiet and isolated. Not a soul knew that she was here, and by now the hunt would be over and the hunters would be riding home to tea. Bay would search for her and not find her, and all the time she was with the man who Bay and Bella had both decided was an outsider; someone she had been told to keep away from.

He flung open a door and their candle flames lit sections of the bedroom and left other parts of it in velvety shadow. He walked across to the fireplace and played his candle flame over the portrait that loomed above the mantelpiece, leaning out from the wall in its heavy carved frame. It showed a running girl, her dress swept sideways into a gale of transparent silk. The dress had a low neckline that left her shoulders exposed, and her hair, yellow as hazel pollen, was twisted away from her brow and secured by a ribbon ... there was a certain wildness to the painting and the girl, something elemental and strange.

'They say she was gazing into a mirror when lightning suddenly came into the room and struck the glass. A shard flew into the girl's throat, just where the main artery beat beneath her bare skin. The parents found her dead when they returned from a seance which the mother had desired to attend. It happened a long time ago, before they came to America and came to live in this house.'

Dina couldn't take her eyes from the portrait, from the stare of the lifeless eyes, painted almost too bright a blue.

'Aren't you afraid of ghosts, *signore*?'

'I'm Latin, so I believe in them.'

'Then——?' She gave a half-gesture, as if to question his wisdom in choosing a house which had been lived in by a couple who would always have been haunted by the sad and terrible memory of their daughter's strange death. It was as if there had been something elemental in the girl, and that some god of the elements had taken her for his own; a dark god desirous of the golden girl with eyes that might have been plucked from among the speedwells.

'I wonder what her name was?' Dina murmured.

'Amarantha, the flower that never fades.'

'How——?'

'I never take anything on chance, Dina. A shrewd gambler always finds out all he can about the game before he decides to lay out his money.'

'I see, so even when you had heard the story you still went ahead and bought the place.'

'I wanted a well-built house, one that neglect might make dusty but not decrepit.' He glanced around, playing candlelight over finely panelled walls that would gleam like dark bronze armour once polish and elbow grease had been applied to them. 'I wanted a bargain, naturally, and I wanted a house in this part of California—not to join your coterie, so don't mistake me, but because there's a certain quality here which hasn't been ruined as yet by the encroachment of the box builder. Had I not bought Adam's Challenge, then your godmother might have had another complaint—that a speculator had moved in and blighted the neighbourhood with his jerry-built bungalows.'

'That's true, Bella felt quite convinced that it would happen and she has already spoken to Bay's father about the possibility.'

'Senator Bigelow, eh? A man of influence for a father-in-law?'

'Yes.' A guarded look came into Dina's eyes and she turned to a table beside the tall-posted bed with its sheeted mattress, and fingered a brocaded box that stood there. She lifted the lid and at once the ghostly bedroom was filled with a tinkling music. Dina didn't recognize the tune, which was in fact *The Floral Dance*. 'Oh, a musical box, and it still plays after all this time!'

'I tinkered with it the other day,' he said drily. 'I imagine that pose of Amarantha was taken from the Floral Dance—she looked as if she danced a lot.'

Dina glanced at the portrait and then back to his face. 'You're charmed by her, aren't you, *signore*? Is that why you aren't afraid of her ghost?'

'It is the memory of her ghost that haunts this house,' he said, 'and I don't think I need fear that she will suddenly appear on the stairs, or facing me at my dining table when I eat alone. In any case she would be a charming visitation, eh?'

'Dancing in through your door to the tune from her musical box. It is an evocative house, but won't you notice how solitary it is when you take time off from your busy life to come and play host to your charming ghost? Or do you plan to bring friends here; business associates and their wives?'

'And become a kind of Gatsby?' he drawled.

93

'Throwing wide my doors to the lively crowd, a man of mystery with a past ... falling in love, perhaps, with a girl of class who belongs to someone else?'

As he spoke he lounged against a tall oaken post of the bed and kept his gaze intently upon Dina's face. She glimpsed the danger in his eyes, like a flame that might suddenly blaze and engulf her.

'I have to go.' She made so quickly for the door that the flame of her candle blew out, plunging her into a pool of shadow. He came to her, tall behind her, and led her along the gallery to the stairs. Dusk had fallen quickly, as it did in the fall of the year, and when they reached the courtyard the sky had turned a deep purple, the colour of nightshade berries.

Dina drew in a deep breath, half of relief, but mostly to take in the evening air, so richly alive with the fragrances of his wild and rambling garden.

'What excuse will you make for being the tardy huntress?' he drawled. 'You won't tell the truth, of course. You won't tell your godmother that you spent time with the man who has been warned never to show his face at Satanita, and when you get safely home you'll wonder how you dared to be alone with him.'

'Yes,' she admitted, almost surprised into the truth because he had led her outside with courtly attention, playing the perfect host to his guest. 'Has no one ever been so good to you that you wouldn't dream of hurting them?'

'Of course,' he said drily. 'I had parents and didn't just arrive in a puff of crimson smoke.'

'Won't they be living here with you? It's a big house.'

'They live in Milan and are happy to be home in Italy.'

'I see. Have you no brothers or sisters?'

'You sound quite concerned for my loneliness,' he drawled. 'My sister Rosaria is married to a Cuban planter and she resides there. My other sister Aragona is a Sister of Mercy in a hospital in Central America. In their separate ways they are happy women with their own lives to lead—they are fully aware that their brother can take care of himself.'

'Are they younger than you, Mr Ventura?'

'By five and six years.' He gave a brief smile, a mere glimmer of white teeth in the gloom of the courtyard. 'Each member of my family has the wish dearest to his or her heart, and so let us leave it at that. Loneliness is a rare thing, or a raw thing. I've been often too busy to assess its possibilities or its pains, and I do assure you that I am not one of your gregarious Italians.'

She smiled a little. 'You've given your family the things they want, and so now you've bought yourself a toy.'

'You could say that—perhaps I should re-name the house Ventura's Toy, eh?'

'Just Ventura,' she said. 'That sounds right to me, with just the right note of—of possession.'

'You were going to say arrogance, were you not?'

'Perhaps.' Her skin flushed in the coolness of the evening air. 'You must be a disconcerting man to work for, the way you worm out one's thoughts with a twist of the pin.'

'My office is known as Dante's Inferno, or so I've

heard it whispered among the staff.'

Chutzpah, she thought. Cool, outrageous nerve, and the electric communication of danger. Anyone who worked for him would have to be on their toes all the time, but it would be exciting, for things would get done, ideas would achieve fruition and like his Sun Tower they would flourish and spread their wings.

'Did you sigh?' he murmured.

'No—perhaps. It's been a strange day, for I never expected it to end this way. I hope you'll be happy in your house, *signore*, with its memories of Amarantha whom the storm god came and took.'

'I'm glad that's how you see it, but you would take the romantic view, eh?' Then, before she could move away and swing into Major's saddle, Raf Ventura placed both hands on her waist and prevented her from moving. She felt a half-frightened thrill at his unexpected touch, something she wanted to prolong and yet pull away from.

'You hoped we wouldn't meet again, didn't you, Dina? No, there's no need to confirm or deny what I say, for we speak without speaking and you know it.'

'Please, Raf, let this be the last time. I've been forbidden to see or talk to you and I obey Bella because she has been truly good to me—my life could have been a disaster without her intervention. She gave me security, and kindness, and she shared Satanita with me. I owe her too much to risk it—in this way.'

Dina could feel the quick beating of her heart as she stood close to Raf's tall, dark figure and felt his strong hands holding her. She wouldn't pull away from him, for that might unleash temper, violence, passion ... it was the passion she most feared, for she didn't know what her own response would be if he started to kiss her.

As she spoke there came the abrupt and painful grip of his hands, pulling her to him until his hard muscles pressed into her.

'Raf ... I'm sure you know women far prettier, far more willing than I am—what is it about me? Why do you do this? Oh, not because of the caviare you had to share with the fishes?' She tried to laugh, but it came out too shakily for that and died into a frightened gasp as he bent his tall head and she felt his breath on her skin.

'Has anyone ever told you, I wonder, that you have sensuous eyes?' Then, in a silence like something in a dream, he laid a kiss against each amber eye, closing them one by one. 'And now I send you home, and whether or not we meet again, *madonnina*, is in the hands of chance.'

'No,' she shook her head at him and the lids of her eyes still felt the pressure of his lips, 'it isn't chance, but you—you have a devil that drives you and I'm afraid of what you'll let that devil do to me. Please, don't wreck my life! Don't make me— hate you!'

'Hating me, or loving me, is not at the command of your will, or mine.' He pressed his hands against her body, and then released her. He unhitched Major and held the stirrup firm while Dina mounted and took the reins.

'You will be safe, riding home alone?' He gazed up at her and now the stars were out she could see the lean strength of his jawline, the thrust of his Roman nose, the black eyebrows above the glint of his eyes.

'Major won't unseat me in the dark woods,' she said. 'I was lost in my thoughts this afternoon, and I think you spooked him.'

'Have you nothing nice to say to me, Dina?'

'Only goodbye, *signore*.'

'Then goodbye, *signorina*. *Addio!*'

Major's hooves rang on the flagstones and she didn't look back ... somehow she couldn't look back to see Raf Ventura standing alone on the steps of the house. His car was there, a gleam of chrome and Roman bronze bodywork, and he would lock up Amarantha's ghost and drive swiftly home to Las Palmas, to his penthouse in the Sun Tower. Their lives had no real meeting point, except for that awareness which had flashed between them, electric as the signalling of the night moths that flew among the dark trees. It held that heady quality attached to the forbidden, except that it wasn't in Dina to take the *dolce far niente* attitude.

Doubtless he could take such an attitude, to enjoy and not worry, but she owed a debt of gratitude and meant to repay it, taking into account the years of good schooling, the pleasurable trips with Bella, and most of all the security that no raffish entrepreneur was going to jeopardise ... his dark fascination had to be swept from her mind.

She and Major left the woods behind them and came out on the sweep of hills that led homeward. Galloping along like this in the magical stillness of the evening, under a skyful of stars, had a keen enjoyment to it that she dared not fathom. The wind was in her hair because she had laid down her hat somewhere in Raf Ventura's house and had forgotten to pick it up, and for a while she seemed to have the world to herself ... Dina the huntress, she thought with a smile, who when she arrived home would have to be ready with a plausible excuse for having deserted the foxhunt, and her fiancé.

Somehow she wasn't surprised when she swung from the saddle in the stable yard at Satanita to be hailed by Bay, emerging from a side door where the light of a wall lantern fell across his face and showed her the anxiety and traces of anger in his eyes.

'Where have you been?' he demanded. 'We've been almighty worried about you!'

'I was unseated,' she handed Major to a young groom. 'My own fault for day-dreaming, and the mettlesome boy trotted off in search of some juicy grass. I had to hunt around for him and before I knew it dusk had fallen. Anyway, we're home safe and sound——'

'That isn't the point, Di.' Bay caught hold of her and hustled her into the house. 'Some of the others noticed you were missing and made a few comments—you don't do these vanishing acts on purpose, do you? You went missing the last time we were out, but only during the kill. This time you really had me worried—I had an image of you being thrown and lying out in the dark somewhere.'

'Oh, the devil takes care of his own,' she said airily. 'Are you staying to dinner? I'm ravenous!'

'Yes, Bella did invite me when I came over to check on whether you were safely back or not. You've lost your hat.' He pushed a strand of gilt hair from her brow and he looked into her eyes as if seeing there a look he had never seen before. Dina wanted to turn away and evade his eyes, but she didn't dare. She felt desperately guilty and prayed that it didn't show ... it wouldn't have been so bad if Raf Ventura hadn't kissed her—the way he had. If he had forced his lips upon hers then she might have been furious, but with a strange and tender audacity, like nothing she had known in her life before, Raf had laid kisses on her eyes and left her with the feeling that they were still there and could be seen.

'I must go and take a shower,' she said, and with a rush of repentance because she had worried Bay, she leaned forward and kissed his cheek. 'Go and pacify Bella for me, and say I'm truly sorry for making her anxious——'

'Anxious is hardly the word!' Her godmother came from the drawing-room into the hall and her painted lips were as thin as knife edges. 'I don't know what has got into you lately, Dina. Instead of behaving like a responsible young woman on the brink of marriage, you go mooning off all by yourself and you cause not only alarm but speculation. Bay tells me that you behaved rather oddly at the country club dance, which I imagine had something to do with that Ventura man. If I thought for one minute that you'd been with him—have you?'

'No!' Dina flung back her head and defied her godmother to call her a liar. 'If you must know the truth, then it's quite simple, and probably ridiculous from your point of view. I can't bear to see a fox or a vixen chased until its lungs nearly burst, when the poor creature is hounded to its death and treated to the final indignity of having its brush removed. The whole procedure sickens me and that's why I ride off, as far away as I can get from the cruelty that poses as a sport. I only take part because I—I like to please you, but I just don't like to see a terror-stricken animal torn to bits by a pack of hounds. I have nightmares about it, but I haven't said anything because—well, in your eyes it's a weakness rather than a strength to be—to have—feelings.'

Bella stood there staring at her white face, and Dina knew that the blood had drained from beneath her skin the moment Bella had mentioned Raf Ventura. It had been a desperate defence to reveal how she felt about fox-hunting, for it seemed as if all her life she had been trying to live up to her godmother's ideals and strengths, and to overcome an innate sensitivity probably inherited from her real mother.

'I've tried to be what you want—sorry.' Dina gave a shrug. 'I guess I'm basically weak-kneed, but you wanted to know.'

'Honey,' Bay was looking a trifle bewildered, 'd'you mean to say you've bottled up all this—this loathing and gone out with the hunt just to please us? You aren't weak-kneed, darling, you're one sweet martyr. Holy hell, why didn't you tell me how you felt? I've never given it a thought because I've had to do tougher things, and I merely regard those little red devils as pests that raid the local farms and orchards. The sweet mystery of you, Dina, takes my breath away!'

'I enjoy the gallop, but that's about all.' Dina forced a smile to her lips, but she could still feel Bella's dark eyes upon her, boring into her, trying to read her mind, still suspicious because she had taken this violent aversion to Raf Ventura and would, if she could, have the hunters out after him for daring to 'raid' her property, on the lookout for a chick he could gobble up, to the last feather.

Dina's smile deepened at the thought, and this seemed to anger Bella.

'What else,' she asked sharply, 'do you force yourself to do in order to please your benefactor?'

Dina's smile vanished. 'Oh, don't let's fall out because I hadn't the nerve to see a vixen being torn apart and sloped off on my own. We can't all have your strength of mind, Bella.'

'No, perhaps not.' Abruptly Bella came to Dina and took hold of her. 'I care a great deal for you and I find it rather hurtful that you should imply that I force you into doing things that go against your feelings. It implies that I bully you. I don't do that, now do I?'

'No.' Dina shook her head ... no, it was all done much more subtly than that and they both knew it. 'Am I forgiven for being a little coward? I know your loathing for the pigeon-hearted.'

'It takes courage to face the guns even if you shake too much to fire one,' said Bay. 'You're okay by me, Di. I only wish you'd confided in me.'

'Do you?' Her amber eyes dwelt on his candid face, with its fairness of skin, carefully shaven and bearing only a few smile lines. 'Perhaps I didn't want to disillusion you, Bay.'

'Honey, I wouldn't want to torment you intentionally.' He grinned.

'You're my gal and I kind of like it that you aren't a bloodthirsty female—why didn't you come and whisper in my ear that you wanted to take a gallop away from the crowd? I'm the guy you're going to marry, so you don't have to mind about dragging me away so we can be alone, Di. Sometimes I think you're a little shy.'

'Oh, you'd have thought me a spoilsport in the

midst of that throng, and the hounds were getting excited so I knew they'd caught the scent of their quarry. I slipped away and it was just a quirk of fate that I got unseated and Major decided to be a bit unruly.'

'No more random adventures, do you hear, Dina?' Bella's hands gripped her slim arms. 'You aren't a schoolgirl playing truant, but a young woman who is soon to be married. Now go and get ready for dinner, and don't keep us waiting.'

'Yes, Bella.' Dina shot a quick look at her fiancé before she made for the stairs and she saw that he was studying her with an intrigued expression in his eyes, as if there was something different about her, some aura that he sensed but didn't fully comprehend. His eyes met hers and her heart gave a jolt, for burning in his pupils was a glow of excitement, as if he would have come for her, had Bella not been present, and caught her in his arms.

Oh lord! Dina dashed upstairs as if hounds were snapping at her heels ... so it did show, that another man had held her and kissed her ... a man who made Bay seem like a nice, kind, athletic boy.

Dina hurried into her bedroom and closed the door behind her. *Oh, stay away from me,* she silently pleaded of that dark stranger, somewhere in Las Palmas, walking tall among his hotel guests in a dinner suit of impeccable cut and style, smiling his brief smile, politely inclining his black head, a man of unfathomable depths and a disturbing, gritty charm.

Please! Dina spoke the word aloud in her bathroom, turning the shower faucet and plunging herself beneath the water as it poured from the chromium showerhead. It streamed down over her slim body, so white in contrast to the indigo-tiled walls, and her face was lifted to the stream in a kind of supplication ... but not every drop in the skies could wipe away the feel of Raf's warm lips as they closed the blue-shadowed lids of her eyes.

Never—never again would she get him out of her senses. She felt the touch of him still, incredibly strong and so vitally alive in every fibre of his body. She had been merely kissed, and yet she felt as if she had been destroyed—he had made her want what she must not even think about.

In a great blue towel she went back into her bedroom and stood there staring at her image in the long triple mirror. It gave back to her a trinity of reflections, of a young woman who looked innocent enough, and yet who had lied to her godmother, and to her fiancé. That hour alone with Raf Ventura had had more meaning than anything which had ever befallen her, and yet it must never happen again. He and his isolated house were out of bounds to her, and if she ever saw him again she must streak off like a vixen and avoid him if she could.

Dina stared into the mirror at her pale, large-eyed face framed by the blue towel, water dripping from her hair and running like tears down her cheeks.

He could tear asunder her heart, her feelings, the entire fabric of her life, and she swore to herself, then and there, that if their paths ever crossed again she would find the courage to turn and run before he ever touched her again with his lean and knowing hands.

In that instant there came a soft knock at her door, jarring her nerves. She swung round, half expecting to see Bella, but it was Chloe, one of the coloured maids, who entered. 'Miz Bella sent me up to help you get dressed for dinner, otherwise you gonna be dawdling again.'

Chloe smiled and walked to the doors of the clothes closet and slid them open. 'Your blue tulle always looks nice, Miz Dina. How about that, or the marble print with them tortoiseshell colours that look good on you?'

'You choose, Chloe. I'm not particular.'

'What, with Mister Bay staying to dinner?' Chloe drew out the marble print dress. 'I see you've got your hair all nice and wet—sometimes, Miz Di, you're like a young gal who won't become a woman.'

'Alice,' Dina murmured, as the maid took diaphanous lingerie from a drawer and laid it on the bed, 'creeping off through the magic mirror to take tea with the Mad Hatter.'

'What's that you say, Miz Di?' Chloe took hold of the towel and began to give Dina's wet hair a brisk rubbing. 'It's a good thing your hair is cut short or we'd never get you ready and Miz Bella would be hopping mad, having a guest and all to dine. A reg'lar one she is for doing things the right way, and you go and get yourself—what's this about taking tea with Alice? Do I know her?'

'I guess we all know her, Chloe. She's somewhere inside all of us, wanting to escape into a world of crazy unreality.'

'Sure, Miz Di, it's a crazy world, but we all got to face up to reality some time or other. You're in a funny sort of mood tonight—I guess you're in love.' Chloe gave her rich laugh as she gave Dina's hair a final rub. 'Now you get dressed and stop your mooning, though I will say he's a handsome young man and you're a mighty lucky gal to have him, what with all them other young ladies angling to catch him. I'll get out them cloudy ambers to go with that dress.'

Dina nodded abstractedly ... in love, Chloe had said, and it was the one thing in the world she didn't dare to be.

CHAPTER FOUR

A FAINT salty breeze was blowing along the beach and there was a refreshing tang in the air. The sun broke the sea into countless golden ripples and the soft high waves pounded the shoreline rocks in ceaseless energy.

Dina lay at her ease on the coolness of the sand beneath a sheltering bush-palm and watched the energetic beauty of the sea through a pair of large-rimmed sunglasses. It was a morning for lazy dreams, when memories flitted in and out of the caverns of the mind like the glimmering fish among the rocks. The beach was long rather than wide and it curved in and out of the coves under the great belt of cliffs, where the seabirds settled like grey and white images, and then flew off again in their everlasting search for food. Dina took a deep breath and felt a primitive response to the mingled scents of ocean salt, seaweed and sunlit sand.

Time and the awareness of everyday life lay beyond the barrier of the cliffs, as if only this place and this moment had any real meaning. The spume leapt high on the pinnacles of rock and the soft thunder of the waves was joined by the buoyant bird calls. Dina felt like some sea creature curled into a shell of peace that was bound to be broken sooner or later, but for now she was safe, nothing had yet come along to prod her out of her enclosure of pleasant sights and sounds. She could have been but a drifting mollusc in her brief shorts and thin cream shirt.

Every secret in the world could be dropped into the ocean, she thought, and then there need be no feeling of guilt; no fear of discovery by those who could be hurt by your secrets. They could lie there in the blue-green depths, safe from the distortions they suffered when they fell into the hands of people who saw only the guilt and never the sadness. Yes, there was a certain sweet sadness to a secret, somehow like the decadent scent in a late summer orchard, or in a room where a lover's flower left its faded perfume.

Dina made a movement with her hand, as if tossing her own secret into the sea ... and then she tensed and stared seaward, and the next instant was on her feet, a cry on her lips.

Someone was out there swimming rapidly towards the shore, and travelling at an angle towards that lone swimmer was the arrow-glint of a lethal fin. Instinct sharp as a claw raked Dina from head to heel and she ran towards the rocks and the spume and the crash of the waves.

'Raf!' She screamed his name even as the waves drowned it. 'Oh God, hurry, hurry, HURRY!'

He could never make it, for sharks were as swift as they were deadly and not unknown along this stretch of the coast, one of the reasons why it was so secluded and why Dina could come here, 'the world forgetting, by the world forgot'.

She was aware of nothing right now but that black head out there, those brown arms cleaving the water, exerting every nerve and fibre in his effort to reach the surge of the waves and be swept into them, thereby confusing that gliding killer who responded to motion and the sounds made by a swimmer.

'Please, God,' Dina prayed, 'let him make it! Just a few more yards and he'll be safe! Dear Christ, I don't ask for anything more than this! I'll never ask for more!'

The waves rolled high, a great silken swirl of water, and when they settled the man was part of them and the moment became so unbearable that Dina couldn't bear it. She flung her hands over her face and waited in a kind of shivering despair. Any second now it would be the shark or the rocks that tore into his body, ripping the brown skin, tearing him apart, turning him from a man to a piece of broken wreckage.

She heard the hammering of her heart and the split-silk sound of the sea as it was gashed on the rocks, and it took all her courage to uncover her eyes and look along the beach.

He crouched there on the sands, dragging air into his lungs, the water streaming off his shoulders, his back, his long legs. 'Raf!' Now she breathed his name. 'Oh, thank God!'

He watched her come towards him, blinking the water from his eyes and shaking it from his hair. The sun glinted on the medallion that he wore around his neck, and Dina knew that sharks were attracted to shiny objects. It was a religious medal, no doubt, for Latins often wore them; the image of some Italian saint engraved upon the gold.

'What were you thinking of?' Her nerves were quivering as if lashed by a storm wave. 'Don't you know how risky this place is for taking a morning bathe?'

'If I'd known, honey, you can bet your bottom

dollar I wouldn't have been tempted.' He sat back on his heels and the lashes clung wetly around his grey eyes as he studied her face, which was icy-white, the pupils of her eyes so expanded they almost blotted out the irises. 'I gave you a scare, eh? Did you know it was me?'

'Th-this is Nun's Cove—I sensed it was you when I saw someone out there, with that shark looking hell-bent for its breakfast. Y-you could be so much chewed-up meat by now!'

'Don't I know it! I once saw a guy torn from shoulder to hip by one of them—hey, don't fall on your face in all this sand!' He leapt and had hold of her ... her fingers clenched a shoulder like warm iron, and his arm was around her waist in a grip of shocking fierceness. 'My sweet noodle,' he murmured. 'The devil takes care of his own, don't you know that?'

All she knew was that he was miraculously alive and in one piece, that by the merest kick of a foot he had escaped those voracious jaws. Whether saint or devil had intervened on his behalf was irrelevant at this moment and all that mattered was being crushed against the firm ribs that caged his heart. She drew a sob-shaken breath.

'After the way you swam you ought to be a contestant for the next Olympics,' she said, and she had to clutch at flippant talk or burst into tears, and she disliked the weak, maudlin self-gratification of tears, which someone like Raf would hate.

'Yes, it was quite a performance for a man of my years.' He touched a finger to the delicate cleft in her chin. 'But I was always as tenacious as Ranjit-sinji, and I'm not easily bowled over. What brought you to Nun's Cove—curiosity?'

'I—I didn't think you'd come here again——'

'That I was more likely to be caught prowling around your private beach, eh? And risk your godmother's withering tongue?'

'You obviously prefer the jaws of a shark,' Dina retorted. 'As I recall Bella didn't seem to wither you.'

'I'm a very tough man, Dina. Didn't you tell me so?'

'I'm convinced of it, after this morning. There wouldn't be much limit to any gamble you might take, for you once told me that you always study the game before making your bid—you knew that sharks had been seen along this stretch of coast and so you decided to test your arrogance against theirs. Isn't that the truth?'

As she spoke Dina gazed up at his strong, life-bitten face, and saw there the hint of recklessness, intensified by the damp strand of black hair across his brow, and the way that danger made his eyes glint. It was even in the feel of his body, as if a dynamo was humming there.

'If life was not a test, a gamble if you like, then it would lose a lot of its excitement. Doesn't a woman take quite a chance when she gives herself to a man—the most elemental challenge of all is the surrender to the emotions, wouldn't you agree?'

'I—I don't think I want to go into all that.' Dina wanted to make a delicate retreat from his arms, but he was unpredictable and she was still shaken by his close escape from the cruel ravages which a shark could inflict upon the human body. 'I'm so angry with you, Raf! You promised to stay away— to leave me alone——'

'It was three weeks ago when we last met, but are

111

you really certain that I made such a promise? I left it to chance, didn't I? I said if we met again it would be by pure chance.'

'Pure!' she exclaimed. 'Is it ever like that, with you and a woman?'

'Dina, is that a nice thing for a well brought up girl to even think, let alone ask?' There was a sunlit mockery in his eyes as they played over her face, and she was desperately aware of how closely he was holding her to his hard body, almost bare except for the damp band of his swimming pants. His warm brown skin was touching hers, and she could feel the tiny nerves quivering inside her as she fought not to react to him, as he wanted to make her react.

'I'm not a fool,' she said. 'I know what you're after.'

'Do you now?' His eyes held hers and for a moment they were conquering, wholly aware of his aloneness with her on this beach that other people avoided; those who liked to be part of the safe jostling crowd, who wanted to fill the water with their carefree antics and rubber rafts overloaded with their noisy children.

'What makes you such a clever girl?' he drawled.

Her skin burned beneath his look, and she felt a twinge of panic at her isolation with him, here in Nun's Cove with its towering rocks like the pillars of a temple and its wild, bird-haunted sweep of cliffs, its seas where the shark lurked.

'A girl doesn't have to be clever to read your mind, Mr Ventura,' she said, frosting her words. 'My godmother told you to stay away from me, so you're out to do the reverse.'

'Out to teach you a little peril, eh? There must

be quite a bit of sweet terror to be wrung from the perils of chastity, and I guess a man like me is fascinated by the terrors a *nice* girl has to hide, not to mention the temptations.'

'Do imagine I'm tempted by you——?'

'Aren't you?' He placed a hand at the nape of her neck and tilted back her head until her eyes were filled with his taunting face ... when she had seen him in the sea and had run across the beach, fear knocking at her heart, she had flung off her sunglasses and they lay somewhere on the sand. She stared up at him and saw the beating pulse under the brown skin of his throat. There was a dark power in his face and body ... he was pagan, sensuous, fearless.

'Don't look at me—so!'

'I like to look at what pleases me. Has no other man ever looked at you and glimpsed the real Dina Caslyn? The young rebel curled inside the shell of cool reserve, longing to find out if love has any real, passionate meaning to it.'

'I don't imagine that you and I would put the same interpretation upon that word,' she said scornfully.

'It isn't a word, Dina, it's a state of body and mind. A longing far beyond a reaching out into the void, where there might be nothing to grasp—not even a dream.'

'What would a man like you want with dreams?' She made herself think of what Bella had told her; forced herself to forget that deadly sensation at the pit of her stomach when she had seen that shark fin cutting towards him in the water. 'You're talking about the sweet swindles of passion, and I wouldn't join that game at the point of a gun.

You'd have to pull the trigger, *signore*.'

'I don't carry a gun, *signorina*.'

'I rather thought you might—as your grandfather did, when he came from Italy and joined a certain notorious gang. Don't bother to deny it, Mr Ventura. My godmother felt it her duty to put me wise about you, especially when it reached her ears that you had bought Adam's Challenge and meant to make it habitable.'

This was Dina's *coup de grâce*. She had been saving it for a moment such as this one, when it became too unbearable to have him touching her and saying things that got right under her skin.

'I see.' His eyes narrowed into slits of pure steel. 'It had to come out, didn't it, especially when a woman like Bella Rhinehart gets out her stiletto. Don Cicero, my grandfather, was a villain, a tzar of the tearing twenties. I don't deny it. But I only knew him as a small child, I rode high on his shoulders and was loved by him. He died, he paid for whatever sins he committed, but my own father was not his sort. We went hungry when he couldn't find work. He brought us up with honour, whether you believe it or not. I don't much care, Dina, what you believe.'

He let go of her then, turned away and watched as the sun caught the wings of a seabird and coated them with silver. Dina bit her lip and couldn't take her eyes from him. He stood tall and immobile, and she felt that he was on the verge of telling her to go to hell, and to take Bella with her.

But instead he gave a cynical laugh. 'Some people never let you forget, do they? My father is a sweet, gentle guy who asks nothing more than to potter about in his Italian garden, growing acanthus, with its silver leaves and crimson petals. And *santolina*, that he trains around the bases of stone pots. Also in his garden there is lavender, lupins and artemisias. And apricot trees. *Cristo santo*, the scent of it all in the hot southern sun! Why don't I go there? Why do I stay and work here, to be called a gangster by an embittered woman for whom luxurious charity has to take the place of a more sumptuous feast? I think I'll go and dress. I left my clothes in that cave beyond those rocks. *Addio*.'

'Raf——'

He paused and looked at her with a sardonic lifting of his left eyebrow. 'You're a protégée for your godmother to be proud of. I congratulate her on a job well done. In a few more years the coatings of ice will be so thick on your flesh and feelings that you'll glitter like a diamond—a lovely frosty diamond with no fire at the heart of you. Keep your cove to yourself, little nun. I wouldn't intrude on you again if you invited me.'

Dina's hand clenched at her left side and she had never felt such a wrenching pain. He would go and it would all be over—but if he stayed it would be a bittersweet wine from a cup that had to be smashed in the end.

'Goodbye——'

The word was on her lips, but when he began to move away, lean and lithe and torn by her instead of that sea brute, she heard something else fly from her throat.

'I have sandwiches and coffee—we could share them. Y-you must feel like a cup of coffee?'

'I feel like I'm kicked,' he drawled.

'I didn't mean——'

'Oh, but you did, Dina. You're so scared to be

yourself that you'll do anything rather than let anyone get to know you. You're like one of those Medici dolls programmed to stab with a very fine needle, poison on its tip. No, I won't share your food, *mille grazie.*'

'Beefsteak sandwiches, and real coffee, not the instant sort out of a tin.'

'Put away your apple, Eve. My name is Ventura and my grandfather died on the island of Alcatraz. I'm untouchable, Dina Diamond.'

'Oh, Raf——' Suddenly she was running to him and when his touch came she gasped as if his fingers were flames. His embrace was fierce, as if he had a need to hurt her because she owed loyalty to everyone but him. For those long moments she felt as if she became part of his vital body, as if they shared the same bloodstream and the same rush of emotions.

When she glanced up at him the audacity was back in his Italianate eyes, half shaded by those black lashes. 'So that's how it happened in Eden, eh? Adam tried to resist.'

'This is all so wrong, so bound for trouble. I—I hated to hurt you.'

'You'll learn in time, Dina. That woman means to make a star pupil of you.'

'Oh, don't let's think about it—let this hour be ours.' As if he opened a vein and let her share his reckless quality, she lifted a hand and touched his cheek. 'You have the kind of face that Dante wrote about—Italian faces are still very Renaissance, aren't they?'

'So are our emotions.'

'I can imagine you riding out with lean hounds and fierce-eyed hawks, across the moors.'

116

'Not across Chicago, with a couple of henchmen and a tommy-gun?'

'That's being unkind.'

'Oh come, Dina, don't tell me you didn't wonder if I was another Don Cicero. Maybe you still wonder, which makes it extra brave of you to fling yourself into my arms. What if I invite you to take a Florida honeymoon?'

'A—what?' She looked at him with wide, uncertain eyes.

'A businessman's amorous trip with his favourite stenographer.'

'Oh—is it on your mind?'

'You put many thoughts in my mind—some of them, whew!' He blew on his fingertips and the edge of his mouth quirked his moustache. 'Do you still want to give me some coffee?'

A nerve flickered in her lip. 'It can only be coffee and sandwiches—you do realise that?'

'No dessert, eh?'

She shook her head. 'I—I hated saying that about your grandfather, but being so scared made me say it. Wanting to talk in this way, and knowing all the time that I shouldn't.'

'The tempting taboo subject of physical attraction,' he said, almost curtly. 'Don't be coy, Dina, about the perils and pleasures that such an attraction can allow or deny.'

'They can't be allowed, Raf. They have to be—denied.'

'All right, don't look so desperate about it. Infatuation has a built-in safety release called disillusion.'

'Am I infatuated with you?'

'Sure. I've crossed over from the other side of the

117

fence and I've made you feel things, like when I was out there and came close to having my legs ripped off. Like when you had to dredge up mud from my past and throw it in my face. I make you come alive!'

'Too much—oh, I'm ravenous! Let's eat!' She pulled free as far as she could, and then gasped as he jerked her back to him, to his body hard with muscle kept rigorously in trim. He drew his lips across her throat, pushing aside the thin shirt to lay bare the mole like a dot of velvet against the smooth skin over her collarbone. His lips were against her bare skin, like the jaguar, she thought crazily, nuzzling her with primitive intention. She edged her face away from his warmth and gazed blindly over his shoulder. The guilty thrill of his mouth touching her was still rippling down her spine, followed by the painful stabbing knowledge that she mustn't give in to this.

'Raf—please——'

'Are you asking for more, or less?'

'Less,' she said faintly.

'So the moon and the dawn can brush against each other but never come together, eh?'

Her silence was her answer, and for a moment everything was dangerously still and quiet between them, the sound of the birds and the sea on the edge of that stillness like a distant thunder.

'Do you trust the grandson of Don Cicero to behave like a gentleman?' he drawled. 'There wouldn't be a soul to witness anything I might do with you, in the Nun's Cove.'

It was true, he had the strength and the ruthlessness, and she could be carried away by what he had called the perils of physical attraction. She felt the tremor deep within her when his fingers slid across her throat, caressing the softness of her skin.

'Don't spoil something I'd like to remember,' she pleaded. 'Don't turn it into something I'd want to forget.'

'Only half an apple for you, Dina?' His tone of voice was quizzical, but his eyes were intent upon her face.

'Eden turned into a desert, Raf, and I wouldn't want that to happen to this place.'

'Our cove,' he drawled, 'and the sea is playing our music.'

Suddenly his arm was strong and warm about her shoulders and he turned her to face the silvery waves breaking on the rocks, splattering spume across the sands to the high reddish cliffs with the sun running down their sides.

His fingers tightened against her and she felt a throb, a flame deep within her. A sweet, forking fire, the awareness of sand under her feet, the sun on her skin, the sea and sky blending together in a pure beauty. She was aware of things, alive to emotions, to joy and tragedy. Within herself she was alike to the sea, fathomless, impenetrable, elemental.

She felt his hand resting on her shoulder like the folded wing of a big bird. 'I'd like you to have this.' His hand lifted and took from his neck the chain and gold medallion. 'I've worn it a long time and it's like something which has been part of me. Have this at least, eh?'

'Oh, but I don't want to break your luck——'

'I make my own luck, Dina. Will you accept the medal? It's stamped with the image of Saint James, patron of the sea, and I'll have pleasure from knowing you are wearing something of mine.'

'If you're sure.' She stood very still and let him pass the fine chain over her head and settle the medal in the V of her shirt. It gleamed against her pale skin and was warm from his body, and there was a kind of significance to the gift, as if he meant her to think of him each time she felt the movement of the medal against her own body.

'Thank you, Raf, but I have nothing to give you in return.'

'You have coffee and sandwiches, haven't you, lady?'

She smiled and they walked across the sands to where her lunch basket lay in the shade of the bush palm. He bent and picked up her sunglasses, and his fingers played with them as he lounged back on the sands with a lazy, tigerish grace of body, a dappling of sunlight across the taut power of his shoulders, catching glints from the sea bloom on his skin. Dina knelt and poured coffee from the flask, the compact food basket being supplied with two of everything so he had a cup, a plate and a fork. Apart from sandwiches there was a salad of tomatoes, crisp leaves of lettuce and sliced red pepper. She shared out the food, giving him the larger portion, and was not unaware of the quirk to his lip when she handed him his plate.

'*Grazie*. The Olympian rewarded for his efforts, eh?'

'Do you often take such fearful gambles?' she asked, sipping her coffee. 'In lots of ways you're a baffling man, aren't you?'

'Most gamblers are—mmm, excellent beefsteak. I believe the redoubtable Bella would have kittens if she could see me right now, sharing her victuals with her goddaughter, who has never looked more attractive, may I say, with tousled hair and shirt, and long bare legs.'

As his glance ran the length of Dina's honey-coloured legs, she knew that it wasn't going to be easy to pull free of his magnetic attraction. *Beware*, cried her instincts. *Beware*, taunted his eyes, and she saw that the tiger wasn't tamed but only putting on a show of being a big cat made lazy by the warm sun.

'I don't think I've ever felt more guilty in my life,' Dina admitted quietly. 'If she ever found out about this picnic—she just wouldn't believe that you have a code of chivalry.'

'Do you believe it, Dina?' His eyes were faintly mocking. 'Don't attempt to disarm me by planting the hero's laurel wreath on my head. I'm just a man, neither saint nor swindler. I can hate like hell if I have to, but on the reverse of the coin— face it, Dina, I'd like nothing better than a dessert of slim silvery-blonde, with eyes the spicy amber of a southern wine. I'd like that so much that I'd advise you not to rely on my so-called chivalry.'

'All the same I'm going to,' she said, with a touch of nervous intensity. 'I'm not a gauche fool, I know you're a man who has led his own life and faced his devils. But there's something—some fine thread of understanding between us that I'd like to weave into my memories.'

'*Santo dio!*' he exclaimed. 'You talk like a woman whose life is behind you instead of just beginning.'

'It begins a new phase when I marry Bay——'

'You don't love him!'

'I do,' she protested.

'Like a brother,' Raf said contemptuously. 'It's

almost a spiritual incest!'

'Don't say such a thing!'

'Don't you care for the truth? What frail flame of excitement flares between you, tell me that? Cheer girl when he aims a chukka, or scores love-fifteen on the tennis court.'

'I'm not going to argue with you, Raf.'

'No, it's always difficult to argue against the truth, and a woman's idea of logic is as scrambled as a bowl of eggs.'

'Thanks. You obviously have a high opinion of the female mind.'

'I have a higher opinion of a female's sense of sacrifice. Is *l'agneau* your pet name at Satanita?'

'Oh—eat your pepper, if you need any!'

'Little fool,' he growled, 'why won't you admit that you're being thrown like a choice bone to that pup, in order to allow Bella Rhinehart to get her teeth into the political pie. She'd love nothing better. A passport into the courts of the senate via her ward's marriage to a Senator's son. What a Brutus she'll make!'

'Oh, do stop it! You're spoiling my lunch.'

'Better to have your lunch spoiled than your life.'

'What nonsense!' She pressed a napkin against her lips in order to hide their trembling; too much of what he said hit too close to a nerve to be altogether bearable. He looked cruel, sitting there with the points of sun and shadow in the dark angles of his face. He didn't know the meaning of compromise, but she had to know it and accept it.

'Marriage to Bay Bigelow would be an impossibility if I compromised you, wouldn't it?'

She stared at Raf. 'You couldn't do that——'

'Want to bet on it?'

'Y-you're just being mean when I hoped you'd be nice—oh, that's a far from possible hope where you're concerned. You aren't a nice man, are you?'

'I never pretended to be, and you shouldn't let the sun get in your eyes so you see a nimbus where there isn't one. Here,' he handed over her sunglasses with a sardonic smile. 'You'll maybe see the real me through a glass darkly.'

'Why,' her fingers clenched the rim of the glasses, 'do you have to be so cynical?'

'Would you prefer me to be sinful? It would be a pleasure, with or without your co-operation.'

'What are you trying to do, Raf? Make me dislike you?' Dina looked at him steadily. 'Is it a defence you put up against people? Are you afraid to let anyone into your stronghold in case they find there a man who can be hurt like everyone else.'

'Honey, I learned a long time ago that the best safeguard is to attack first, and it's a rule I live by in business and pleasure. That's what makes the shark so formidable; he doesn't stop to wonder if it's going to be painful when he snaps his jaws and takes off a leg.'

'Please, don't remind me of that!' Dina flinched from the mental picture he evoked. 'So that's your philosophy—don't be afraid to be ruthless, and don't ask for pity if and when the tables are turned and you lose the game?'

'There you have it, as neat as a nut in its shell.' His lips moved in a brief, lopsided smile. 'Look at it from my angle. I find a house I like, so I go ahead and buy it, and I send in the builders to make repairs, and the decorators will follow to make things spruce. And what happens? Your godmother gets to hear that the house is sold and about to be occupied, and that would be dandy, so long as the purchaser wasn't someone like me. A self-made Italian–American, who must be crooked because way back in his family there was an immigrant who arrived in the States at the time of the depression and was unable to find a steady job, so he joined a bootlegging gang. Unfortunately he was shrewd and a natural leader and one day he found himself in charge of things; the money was good and he'd never had any before—well, it's in the past and it should be forgotten, and maybe forgiven as he paid the ultimate price for his sins. But no! The word is out that Raffaello Ventura is the new owner of the Penrose mansion, and the rulers of the roost are going to try and put me to flight.

'Try is the operative word, and I don't doubt that Bella Rhinehart will use every trick in the book to try and prove that I'm an unsavoury character, playing St Georgia for all she's worth, and maybe getting hoist on her own poniard if she isn't careful. I can fight below the belt if I have to, and it wouldn't worry me to tilt that arrogant woman right on her nose, in a patch of front-yard dirt she has managed to sweep under the rose trees, until it's become part of their perfume.'

Dina found herself looking at a dark and menacing face, and feeling the thrust of his words like so many sharp little knives. 'You could have bought a house anywhere,' she said. 'Pasadena isn't the only attractive region of southern California, and it must be costing a great deal to put that old place in order. Why come here?'

'Why not?' His eyes flashed, and he leaned forward so that his right arm formed a formidable bar across Dina's body, supported by his hand, the fingers tensile in the sand. 'I've earned the right to live wherever I choose, and no *grande dame* is going to dictate to me, or attempt to discredit me. She doesn't scare me, Dina. She doesn't have to scare you.'

'I'm not——'

'Aren't you? Right now you're on edge and wondering if she has a crystal ball up there at Satanita, into which she gazes and sees everything that goes on.'

'I won't listen to you—Bella's been generous and good to me, and she cares about my future. Girls are only a passing pleasure for you—all you want is to make another conquest, and all the better if it's someone like me. I offer a bit more challenge because I'm not the sort of blonde you're used to—to picking up!'

'Honky-tonk gals, with the dark roots showing through the blonde hair, eager for a good time and happy to pay the price?'

Dina flushed at the sarcastic edge to his voice, and her answer was to tilt her chin in defiant acknowledgement of what he said.

'You consider yourself way above that kind of girl, don't you, Dina?' As he spoke he moved his hand until it touched her cap of silvery hair, softly shaped and still as fair as when she had been an infant of three, transported from a Los Angeles apartment where all the furniture had been removed by the brokers' men, and brought in a limousine to a grand house with bougainvillaea cloaking its boundary walls.

'And yet, Dina,' his voice seemed to cut into her, 'you might well have been one of them. That's where Bella came in, eh? She took you on because there's no doubt in the world that you were a beguiling kid, and she brought you up, and made sure she enslaved you. She can do as she pleases and you'll concur, even if she throws mud at me until it clings and other people start to agree that crookedness is bred in the bone, and I'm a dangerous man to have in the vicinity.'

He moved nearer to Dina, until she felt the pressure of his arm, forcing her almost into a recumbent position on the sands. 'You won't raise a whimper of protest, will you, even though I could hold you in my arms right now and make you want me until you cry out with it.'

'Raf—don't!' Her eyes looked up into his, and she felt the turning of her heart as she caught the ruthless glint in his eyes. 'You're deliberately spoiling what we could have had——'

'And what is that, pray?'

'Friendship—oh, it isn't to be sneered at and you know it. You aren't a man to go around making friends all over the place; you just don't trust people enough for that. But we seemed to establish a kind of rapport.'

'And on the basis of that were you planning to be Daisy to my Gatsby?' He laughed softly and at the sound and its infinite irony Dina arched away from him, inadvertently bringing his face forward against her bare throat.

'Little Miss Chastity,' he mocked, 'guarded like the sacred flame until you have it quenched in the arms of the chosen youth, all blue blood and calf muscles like tennis balls.'

'You—you're no gentleman,' Dina flung at him, struggling in his arms with the desperation of a young animal with a tiger breathing down her neck.

'One doesn't struggle out of a Chicago ghetto by always behaving like a gentleman,' and quite deliberately he drew the edge of his moustache across her skin. 'Mmmm, sweet—they made you out of flower petals and honey, didn't they?'

'I wish I'd let you walk away,' she panted, twisting back and forth in an effort to avoid his mouth. 'I wouldn't have felt any compunction if I'd known you'd turn into some kind of—of savage!'

'It's what you need, *donna mia*, to be woken out of that enchanted sleep of yours before it's too late.' His lips came down to take her mouth and with all her might Dina brought up her right knee and slammed it into him. His hands ground into her and she saw the shock of pain register in his eyes, then he groaned and rolled away from her and lay there in the sand with the muscles of his back as taut as straps.

Dina leapt to her feet, choking a sob with her fist. She had been shown how to do that in her final year at school, but she hadn't dreamed that it could be so effective, and so agonising for the man involved. She had felt her knee sink into him, and nothing had mattered in that split second except that he didn't put his mouth to hers and justify every suspicion that lurked in every cell of her body ... that she wanted him as she had never wanted the man she was going to marry ... wanted everything blotted out in the sheer immolation of sensual fire and forgetfulness.

And there he lay, over on his back now, gazing up at her with eyes like a diamond drill.

'Desperate little bitch, aren't you?' he said. 'So

you, too, can hit below the belt when you have to.'

'You drove me to it.' She couldn't endure his eyes and desperation clutched her heart that it had to be ended, once and for all. 'You talk about people ruining my life—my father was ruined by one of your sort! Leave me alone! Keep out of my way, and don't ever put your hands on me again!'

'Why, do you know karate as well?' he drawled.

'Go to the devil, Raf!' White-faced, doing what had to be done, Dina flung utensils into the lunch basket, uncaring of the coffee dregs in the cups and the remnants of salad on the plates. She snatched up her flamingo-coloured rug, and she fled ... fled unchased to the rough steps cut into the side of the cliffs and winding all the way to the top. She didn't pause until she arrived on the bluff, where the beat of the sea was carried upward to merge with the pounding of her heart. Tears streaked her face and she ached deep down where she had kneed Raf, and half-blinded she made for her coupé, parked at the side of the road beyond the wide grass verge.

She sat inside the car and it was several minutes before her tears and her nerves were under some kind of control. She wiped her face with a tissue and stared at herself in the front-view mirror. God, she couldn't go home in this state, and with a trembling hand she combed her hair and put some colour on her lips. As she straightened the collar of her shirt her fingers came into contact with the medallion which Raf had given her.

For a wild moment she was tempted to wrench it off and throw it from the car, into the long grass where it would tarnish. Her fingers clenched the medal and she felt the graven image upon it ... nothing was left but this disc of gold and the wounding memory of Raf lying there on the sands with that cold, awful smile in his eyes.

She had made him hate her, Dina felt convinced of that. She wouldn't see him again to be tormented by these feelings that were so disloyal to Bay. The sun reflected in the diamonds of his ring as she turned the ignition key and started the car. There was nowhere to go but home ... and yet she couldn't face it, walking into Satanita as if nothing had happened and she had spent a quiet, relaxed morning on the beach. She felt like a coil of nervous energy and she just had to unwind or snap, and that unwinding process couldn't take place at home, not if she ran into Bella. Her godmother was too adept at reading her moods and she would instantly guess that Dina was all tensed up and that someone had caused that tension. She would start asking questions and Dina dreaded giving away the answer without even breathing the man's name. Now Raf Ventura had bought the old Penrose house, Bella knew that he was in and out of the district, and she was furious enough already that he had dared to buy property not all that far removed from Satanita itself.

It would be unendurable if she guessed that another traumatic meeting had taken place between Dina and that 'damned racketeer' as she called him, and with a set jaw Dina drove past the incline that led homewards and made for the country club. A couple of hours of activity might help her to regain her balance, and there would be bound to be someone at the club who would agree to a few sets of tennis. It was a game Dina liked and she was quite a good player, but more than that she needed the physical effort that might dull the vivid pain of her thoughts.

Even as she drove through the sunshine along the well-kept drive of the club, she felt as if she were driving through the black heart of a storm. A torn section of herself had been left behind on that beach and there was no going back to reclaim it.

As luck would have it the tennis professional was on the courts when she arrived there and he said at once that he'd be happy to give her a game. He was a lean, good-natured man, and not being a close friend he didn't make personal conversation and Dina was able to throw herself into the game without the need to put on her usual show of the bright, lucky bride-to-be of the club's most favoured young buck. She could slam hard at the ball and leap back and forth in an energetic effort to daze herself of thought and feeling.

At the end of the first set, as they changed sides, her partner gave her a grin of approval. 'On that showing, Miss Caslyn, you could enter for the amateur cup. Your game has improved remarkably—I had no idea you were this keen.'

'I guess I'm in the mood of the game,' she replied, forcing a smile. 'And you play so well, Jack, that I'm bound to try and keep up with you.'

Keep up she did, until there was only the hard smack of the ball across the net, the sting of the hard court under the soles of her feet, and the feel of perspiration drying cool on her warm skin. She was beaten in the final set by a hard driving ball from her sinewy opponent, and her smile was effortless this time, as she shook his hand.

'Many thanks, Jack. That was a game of a lifetime.'

'I must say I enjoyed it.' He narrowed his eyes as

he took in her flushed face and tousled hair, the shorts and shirt that gave her a slightly boyish air. 'As the winner by a fluke, let me invite you to a lemonade on the terrace, Miss Caslyn?'

'Why—yes, I'd like that.' They walked together to the steps that led up to the terrace, and Dina felt at ease with the man because their talk was of tennis and some of the champion players he had been matched against, both here in California and abroad. 'I guess one of the great sportsmen, and one of the nicest, was Fred Noble, the English champion,' he said, as they sat drinking iced lemonade through straws. 'It was a great pity about him, you know. He had some fearful luck with one of his legs and was forced to retire from the game at the height of his fame. He had inimitable style, had Fred Noble. The way he walked on to the court, the way he grinned at the crowd, and was he modest! It can't be said of all champs that they show that degree of charm and modesty.'

Dina spent a pleasant half hour with the professional, and after he had left she sat on in the shade of the terrace, half concealed behind her sunglasses, no longer so tensed up that each nerve in her body felt as if it were a tiny screw which had been driven too tightly into her frame.

The passing of time had become irrelevant and the sun was declining across the courts when several couples sauntered out from the clubhouse to play tennis in the cooling, fragrant air, softly alive with bird calls and the scent of the shrub flowers that were lifting their heads now the heat of the day was abating.

The fine weather was lingering far into September ... the thought broke off jaggedly in Dina's mind and she leaned forward, disbelief in her eyes as she stared downward at one of the courts. For seconds on end she couldn't believe the evidence of her own clear sight, and by the time one' of the men had twirled his racket and won the toss for the side that didn't face the setting sun, Dina had recognised him too vividly to be able to move from her seat. Her every muscle felt rigid, her ankles were clamped as if by invisible irons, and all she could do was remain there and watch the set.

The unbelievable matching of her fiancé, facing the red-gold shaft of the sun, against the man she had left on the sands of Nun's Cove, his eyes as cold and sinister as those of a tiger shark.

Her heart gave a tormented throb ... he wouldn't let it end at Nun's Cove. With his sense of diabolical irony he would find a way to hurt her, and his attack would be far more subtle than hers had been.

She sat there as if bound in chains and couldn't take her eyes off him as he played against Bay, whom he must have challenged some time during the day. It was well known that Bay was proud of his sporting abilities, and Dina had already learned that Raf Ventura could make things happen, like some dark sorcerer from the Medici era. He had probably telephoned Bay and made a bet that would involve a large cheque to some charitable fund of Mrs Bigelow's, and there was a boyish side to Dina's fiancé that found a challenge irresistible.

Damn him! She felt right now that she hated that long, lean opponent of Bay's, clad in shirt and ducks that gleamed white in the almost satanic glow of that powerful sunset. He had a long sure reach, with a spring to his feet that was almost

132

animal, and a quickness of reaction that made his partner leap all over the court in an attempt to counter the swift-flying ball from across the net. Dina watched the way he served the ball, with a slicing backhand drive that had a deadly quality about it.

Raf was playing as if he meant to slaughter the man she was going to marry, and she silently prayed that Bay would not be beaten. It was awful, the trouble he was having in meeting and driving back those shots that whizzed at him like—like so many arrows fitted with warheads that were striking through his guard and his poise.

Suddenly an irresistible impulse overcame Dina and at the same time her ankles were free of those shackles which shocked surprise had locked about them. She left the terrace and ran down the steps that led to the tennis courts, and she joined the bevy of club members who had drifted over to watch the match, attracted by the exciting momentum of the game, and by the fact that one of the club's best players was matched against a man who was obviously a stranger to them.

Dina caught the murmurs of inquiry as she stood there, and then quite deliberately she moved her position to the side of the court, until Raf Ventura couldn't avoid seeing her. She caught the flash of his eyes and saw the sudden way he was thrown off his stroke, so that he missed the ball as it came flying across the net.

A quick smile lit Dina's face and she willed her fiancé to make a comeback to his usual excellent form. Bay had seen her as well and knew that she was there to cheer him on, and from the moment he caught sight of her he strove to match his skill against Raf Ventura's less polished but powerful use of the racket.

Had there been no personal feeling involved in this match, Dina might have enjoyed such a display of stamina, and the sheer excitement generated by two men who were battling for supremacy like a pair of gladiators in a Roman arena ... one of them must suffer defeat and it looked as if they'd kill each other before the conclusion of the match.

'Wow!' exclaimed a girl who stood not very far from Dina, 'I've never seen Bay Bigelow pressed this close to the ground. Who is that guy he's playing against—look at the way he shows his teeth! My, what teeth, white and biting as a wolf's!'

Dina gazed through the gathering dusk at Raf Ventura; his teeth were bared against his dark skin, and glittering in his eyes was a devil light. He was having the time of his life, for he knew, as she did, that his ruthless strength would defeat her fiancé, and the image of him sauntering off that court with a sardonic smile of victory on his lips was like gall on her own mouth.

She could let him win, or she could go to the club secretary and inform him that a non-member of this exclusive club was using a facility provided for members only ... instead Dina suddenly turned away from the contest and made for the parking lot. She drove home to Satanita feeling as if a stiletto was pricking her heart ... she was nothing but a little coward who had run out on Bay and left him to be swiped all over that court by a merciless man who used her fiancé as a reprisal. He would win and walk away, and make sure later on that Bay's friends got to hear that he had been beaten by the *restaurateur* who supplied the club bar and buffet with food and drink.

Dina felt as if she had been out on that court herself, untidy, tousled, and nervously torn, but as luck would have it Bella had gone out to dine, and the staff already knew that Dina was content to have a modest meal in the *sala* when she ate alone.

She wasn't terribly hungry and had an omelette to offset the sinking feeling deep inside her, and afterwards, unable to shake off her feeling of depression, she flung a jacket about her shoulders and took a stroll in the garden. She had never needed the tranquillity and the night-time fragrances quite so much, and she wandered along the avenues of trees, and up and down small flights of stone steps that led to arbors and hideaways which she had known from a child.

She sought to find her lost contentment, but it was as if she had lived through a tempest and now that everything was quiet again she couldn't adapt to the stillness and felt that at any moment the storm would come sweeping back.

An hour passed in this way and Dina was in the gazebo, which was perched upon an eminence that in daylight overlooked a small valley filled with multi-coloured azaleas, when a shadow passed by the window where she sat.

The shadow paused in the doorway. 'Chloe said I might find you in the garden.'

Dina had known a moment almost of terror and when Bay stepped into the gazebo she flung herself forward and threw her arms about his neck. 'I hated to run out on you, but I—I just couldn't endure any more of that hateful game!'

'Hush, Di, it's all over. The game sort of went my way after you left—he seemed to run out of fire and we finished with the honours even.'

'I wanted you to win—so badly.'

'Darling, why take it so much to heart? It was only a bit of sport.'

'Sport? It was like watching a dogfight, seeing who could snap closest to the bone.'

'You *are* intense about it!' Bay put a kiss against her brow, and with a sudden contriteness, a strange guilt drawn from the depths of herself, Dina turned her lips to his and kissed him with a rare fervour.

'I wish we were married, Bay——'

'I wish it too, honey, but we have to wait while Mam and Bella enjoy themselves with the trousseau, the invitations, the plans for our trip through Europe, the organ music and the cake. We can't spoil their fun, Di, not when we mean so much to them.'

'The thought of all that show is giving me the horrors,' Dina said tensely. 'I wish we could just do what lots of other couples do. Jump into a car and head across the border into Mexico and be married there, quietly and quickly, with no fuss at all.'

'I'd like that as well, darling, but I can't disappoint Mam.' He placed a kiss against Dina's left ear. 'Being an only child has its responsibilities, and once all the preliminaries are over you'll love being a white bride, all glowing and silky and carrying a long spray of those bell-mouthed lilies. You'll look great, Di. I'll be the envy of every other guy—say, you do seem in a fond mood tonight,' as her arms tightened about his neck, 'and there was I thinking at times that you weren't a girl to go all that crazy over the idea of marriage. I don't really know you, do I, Di?'

'Of course you know me, Bay.' She said it with more conviction than she felt. 'Why, we met when I was thirteen and you were sixteen and your mother invited me to your birthday party. I can remember how thrilled Bella was.'

Yes, thought Dina, thrilled because at last those clouds hovering over her infancy had finally rolled away and Senator Bigelow's wife had decided that the slender schoolgirl with the fair shining hair was a suitable person for her son to associate with. Bella had taken her into Los Angeles to buy a special dress for the party and an expensive gift for Bay. Her plans had been laid that day and firmly built upon ever since, and the culmination would be the joining in matrimony of her goddaughter and the most eligible young bachelor for miles around. A young man who had birth, breeding and good looks, and money of his own settled on him by his grandfather.

I want to be thrilled, Dina cried out inside herself. I want to be wildly, romantically in love. I want to feel *something* when I think of being married.

'Come along, honey, it's time you were tucked up in your little wooden bed.'

'I'm not a child, Bay!'

'Whoever suggested that you were?'

'You—the way you're talking to me, as if I have to be pacified because I hated that slamming match between a pair of grown men trying to prove their superiority. Men are the ones who behave like overgrown kids at times!'

'Okay, so it was a crazy kind of game, but Ventura phoned me and made this bet and I wanted to beat him, especially when I remembered what Bella said about him, that he had bought the Penrose place with bent money.'

'How do you know it's bent?' Dina demanded. 'I don't suppose his money is any more dirty than anyone else's—oh, why can't Bella let sleeping dogs lie? She, of all people, to drag skeletons out of closets when I have mine.'

'What the heck are you talking about?'

'The way my father lost his money, and the way he lived on the beach, soaked in wine until one day he vanished into the sea. It was never a secret. Bella took me in and made me acceptable to your sort.'

'Oh sure, my sort. We're not saints.'

'I'm glad to hear you admit it.'

'But there's something about Ventura that gets under my skin like a niggling grit. A sardonic air of seeing through you, as if he has radar eyes and has lived while I've been playing with my kiddy car. You don't like him either, Di, that's for sure.'

'No—I don't like him,' she said quietly.

'Then let's forget about him. I guess if Bella has her way he'll have things made so thorny for him hereabouts that he'll be glad to sell up and go elsewhere, to act the fake gentleman.'

'Fake is hardly the word.' Dina couldn't have prevented herself from making that objection had she tried.

'Then what is the word?'

'He has what Latins are born with and what other men have to acquire.'

'Is that so?' A stiff note came into Bay's voice. 'Do enlighten me on what this Italian café owner has that I haven't got.'

'The audacity to be himself,' she replied. 'Shall we now make tracks for my little wooden bed—

which really isn't so little, being a Queen Anne fourposter which Bella had shipped over from England.'

'Do you know, Di, you sounded—almost provocative.'

'Did I?' Her smile was fleeting and left a curious ache on her lips. 'Well, you said you didn't quite know me, didn't you, Bay? But do any of us truly know ourselves?'

'Maybe not, but there's something I'd place a high bet on, something you have, honey, that went out with button-up shoes when it comes to a lot of other girls these days.'

'And what is that, Bay?'

'Virtue.' He said it in a kind of tight-lipped voice, and Dina had an idea that he blushed; it was too dim in the gazebo to really make out more than the gleam of his eyes.

'Virtue,' she echoed. 'Is it the jewel that you prize above a skeleton in my closet?'

'I guess I do,' he said gruffly. 'That skeleton has very little to do with you, Di. You were a small, sweet kid and quite innocent of anything your father did.'

'Yes,' she murmured . . . and so had Raf Ventura been a small kid, innocent of knowing that the kind, laughing man who carried him on his shoulders was in reality Don Cicero, a leading figure in the underworld of Chicago in the twenties.

Distant events did cast their shadow, she thought. Making what Scott Fitzgerald had called a 'dark night of the soul'.

Yes, that was what she carried like a scar, and what Raf carried—a dark shadow on the soul. People sensed it in him because he was so dark to look at, but her fairness of skin and hair was a camouflage that she wore like the chameleon.

On the day of her marriage she would wear glistening white satin and carry ivory-white lilies, and no one would really suspect that her heart was where it shouldn't be ... high on a sun tower, warming itself at a forbidden flame.

'May I kiss you?' Bay asked suddenly.

'Of course.' She lifted her face like an obedient child and only her lips felt the touch of his mouth ... the rest of her was fathoms deep in pure ice, cool, unmelting, as she slipped in and out of her fiancé's gentle arms.

He didn't question the cool reserve of her response; for him she was a girl of virtue and that above all was what Bay Bigelow had been reared to prize and desire in his bride-to-be, along with enough charm of face and person to make him the envy of his peers. He didn't expect, let alone want, a desperately ardent fiancée. He had been taught that a lady didn't show her feelings, and as he and Dina strolled in the direction of the house, her arm was tucked within his, and her feelings were known only to herself.

CHAPTER FIVE

IT had never occurred to Dina that there might come a time in her life when she would feel so unsettled that when she slept she had curious dreams that woke her at dawn, when she would rise while a mist still lay over the grounds, to saddle Major and ride the devils out of her system, and so be ready to face the day ahead of her.

No one guessed that she was holding a tight rein on a secret self that clamoured to break free of all the ritual and the eager preparations for her wedding day.

The day when she would become for always the property of these people who saw her as the perfect bride, who would become the charming young hostess of the house that was to be built on a plot of land on the Bigelow estate, and there with Bay found a small but agreeable family.

The preparations had now reached their peak and fitting for the lovely satin dress had begun. The glimmering material for the gown had come from Ceylon, where it had been entirely woven by hand, yards of it, providing enough for a train that would be edged by some beautiful Austrian lace which Bella had never used. Slippers to match the dress were being hand-made at a shop in Hollywood that catered for some of the screen's most glamorous stars.

Dina felt as if this were a production rather than a wedding, but she maintained an outward calm and managed to sail through the first fittings without a sign of the inward strain that she was feeling and which broke her sleep into strange eddies of fact and fiction.

There was never a shadow of doubt in her mind that she would go through with the marriage, but it would have been so much easier to face had Bay agreed to an elopement. To leave behind all the fuss and bother and with a special licence in his pocket to drive across the border and be the participants in a service that would be quick and witnessed by strangers who wouldn't stare and whisper, and gush compliments all through the reception.

But Bay was devoted to his mother, and being an only child he felt it his duty to provide her with the fulfilment of a real wedding day, one she could look back upon with pride, with all the correct and proper trimmings such as a towering iced cake that would be cut with the sword which a Bigelow had carried into battle during the war between the States, the delicious slices enjoyed with champagne from one of the best cellars in France. Photographs would be taken to be placed in an album specially made and stamped with the family name, and not forgotten would be the ritual of the bridal bouquet being thrown to the bridesmaids just before the happy couple sped away on the first lap of their honeymoon.

It seemed more like the wedding of Bella and Mrs Bigelow, for their excitement far outshone Dina's ... the single relief of those hectic days was the postponement of her godmother's vendetta with Raf Ventura. Bella had far too much to think about, and the culmination was that on the afternoon of a crucial fitting she developed one of her migraine headaches, which Dina knew to be painful to a high degree, with a needlepoint of agony starting at the temple, blurring the vision, and then producing a spinning disc of light that cut objects into two. It was a swimming effect that could only be alleviated by complete rest in a darkened room, but when Dina offered to stay and be a comfort to her godmother, Bella became agitated and insisted she attend the dress fitting, the last one before it was finally sewn and the train was attached.

'I don't like to leave you like this——'

'Do go,' Bella pleaded. 'You know how much I want everything to be just right, and the dress is so important—oh, the devil take this headache! Why did it have to happen just now?'

'Because you've been hustling and worrying and getting yourself all tired out.' Dina bent over her godmother and pressed a kiss to her cheek, which felt feverish. 'Try to sleep, dear.'

'Dina.' Bella clutched at her with hot, dry hands. 'I've never told you this before, but I had feelings for your father that were more than fond, and I was in despair when he made such a wreck of his life. I don't want anything like that to happen to you, and Bay is such a nice boy, with good blood in him and the ingrained instinct to always do the honourable thing. He'll make you a fine husband and in time you'll have few regrets.'

'Oh, Bella, what regrets could I have——?'

'Do you think I'm blind, Dina? I've caught a look on your face at times which has caused me more concern than you might realise. I know that young girls dream of a romance that sweeps them off their feet and makes everything seem enchanted, but it just doesn't last. It's only in films that the snow falls without turning to slush, and where the icing shines on at the end of the story. Believe me, you'll have something far more substantial than a dream. You'll have position, security, and none of the heartache that romantic love can cause. You'll be part of a dynasty, for the Bigelows are among the founders of California, and their family tree is a solid one. You see, my dear child, we don't stay young and idealistic, we grow older and we learn that reality has firmer foundations than the raptures of youth. I have to be wise for you—you do see that?'

The feverish fingers clung to Dina's. 'You're Lewis's daughter and his streak of instability has always worried me in case it showed in you—you will abide by my wishes? You'll marry Bay no matter what devil whispers in your heart that he'll never be a wild and impetuous lover? Oh, this damned head of mine! I—I'm seeing lightning——'

'Do relax, Bella, or the migraine will get worse.'

'Promise me——'

'I never break my promises, you know that.'

'You never have, but lately there's been a subtle change in you. Is it that man?'

'No!' Dina felt shocked, as if someone had hit her across the windpipe, for there was no question in her mind that her godmother referred to Raf Ventura.

'I know he's unsettled you, and it's psychological—Lewis was ruined by that kind of man——'

'I don't plan to be ruined by any man.' Dina had to force some lightness into her voice or have an attack of the kind of despair that the Tolstoy novels were full of. 'I'm off for that fitting you're so concerned about, and I'll call in at Royal and Weale to see if my satin slippers are ready. If so I can bring them home and you'll soon get better so you can see them and make sure they're exactly as you wished them to be.'

'Am I being a despot?' Bella asked. with a slightly pathetic note in her voice that was quite out of character. 'It's just that I want everything to be perfect, so that long afterwards people will remember your wedding and say how matchless it was. I—I want nothing to go wrong—you'll go straight to the fitting, see about your slippers and come directly home?'

'Of course I shall. Now close your eyes and go to sleep, and when you wake up the pain will be gone.'

'You're a good child, but don't dawdle—that fitting is at three o'clock.'

'I'm off! 'Bye!'

Today that early mist had developed into something more opaque, and it had not dispelled itself by the time Dina arrived at the fashion house. She travelled in the elevator to the third floor and was greeted at once as a valued client, and she spent the next hour being fussed over and fitted into the almost completed dress.

It was undeniably lovely, being almost gothic in its simplicity of line so the glimmering material was shown off to advantage, as would be the necklace of diamonds she would wear on the day of the wedding. Dina found the train a trifle cumbersome, but her bridesmaids would cope with that, so she didn't say anything. She smiled and nodded and was as serenely agreeable as she had been throughout her 'ordeal' as she secretly thought of it.

It was an intense relief when she finally made her escape from the scented, almost precious atmosphere of this shrine to fashion, being escorted to its doors by the designer of her dress.

'Nevaire 'ave I been so delighted with a garment I design from my own 'ead,' the little Frenchman assured her. 'Like Punch I am pleased and I 'ope that the so charming Mees Caslyn is also 'appy?'

'Stunned is the word, *monsieur*,' and she stood there while he kissed her hand and stared at her ring as if assessing its glittering value down to the last centime.

'You will make a dazzling bride,' he told her, and his smiling teeth were unnaturally white under the dark moustache that was as slender as an actress's eyebrow. 'Nevaire 'ave I seen skin and 'air as fair as yours, Mees Caslyn. They are natural, *hein*, and not from the bottle as is too often the case in this city of 'ollywood.'

'You're more than kind to say so, *monsieur*, and now I have another appointment——' Dina moved her hand within his. 'I don't want to be late.'

'Ah, thus it is with a bride-to-be, dashing from one place to another. Do wish upon your good *tante* my desires that she soon be well again.'

'Indeed I shall. *Au revoir, monsieur!*'

'*Au revoir*, Mees Caslyn, and do be careful how you drive in the smog which seems to 'ave come down a leetle thicker. Bah, what stuff, and so trying to the eyes!'

'Yes, isn't it?' Dina hurried away, making for the

boulevard where the shoemakers Royal and Weale were situated, and she saw the mist quivering in the crowns of the palm trees and twisting like faint silver ribbons around their sculptured trunks. There seemed to be a faint husky whispering in the upper air, and Dina was gazing upwards when she walked right into someone and felt herself grasped by hands like steel claws.

'I am sorry—oh!'

Dina stiffened as if electricity had gone through her. She was confronted by a man in a tan safari suit with brown trimming, and as she stared at him a jet sliced its way through the white mist overhead and its roar was in her head and she felt dizzy for a moment, as if she might fall over.

I fled him, down the nights and down the days ... and then she was aware again, with all her senses strung on fine quivering wires inside her motionless body, concealed behind her pale mask of a face. To other pedestrians passing by they were a man of singular darkness and a young woman of striking fairness ... they didn't know that Dina had just walked into the devil's web.

'What an unexpected surprise,' he said, that curiously attractive rasp in his voice that had sawn into her, the last time they had been together. He smiled and half-bowed and both actions were infinitely sardonic. Dina stood speechless, remembering acutely the pain which she had caused him ... now he was the image of the suave man about town, his hair like a black casque above his dark distinctive features ... only when she looked into his brazen, dangerous eyes did he let her know that nothing was forgotten between them, least of all that she was a girl on the threshold of marriage to another man.

'I—I'm on my way to see if my—my wedding slippers are ready,' she said, and her voice sounded as strained as a schoolgirl's.

'You thought you'd be in time, eh?' he drawled. 'Well, if you're bound for Royal and Weale then I'll walk along with you.'

'No, Raf.' She backed away from him, almost into a pram that a young nursemaid was pushing along. Raf reached out and caught at Dina's wrist, holding her steady. She flushed and looked at him with pleading eyes, but nothing softened in his face; his eyes were like steel, to match his fingers holding her.

'You can hardly stop me, Dina. I'm on my way there to pick up a new pair of riding boots, and it would be a trifle infantile to go single file when we can keep each other company. What's the matter? Do I embarrass you?'

'Of course not—and do stop holding my hand! Someone might see us a-and you know how people talk.'

'Yes, what a meaty little bone for the scandal cats to get their teeth into.' His smile was the essence of mockery and careless disregard for what anyone thought of him. 'But tell me, do you really care what that kind of person thinks?'

'No—at least, I care that my behaviour doesn't damage Bay's good name in any way.'

'And being seen with me is likely to damage it?'

'You'd revel in it,' she rejoined. 'You tried to wipe the tennis court with him and found it wasn't so easy.'

'My dear Dina, the game lost its zing when you chose to run away—do you always turn tail and run when the game hots up? Are you going to try it on right now?'

'You aren't going to let me, are you?' Her fingers moved helplessly within his. 'Oh, do let's walk along! We're attracting attention!'

'You sound nervy, very much on edge,' he said, as side by side they proceeded along the pavement to the shoemaker's, an overcrowded, leathery shop where some of the most affluent and famous feet in Hollywood were skilfully measured for hand-tooled shoes, boots and sandals made from the finest hides. That Raf should be a client of the shop didn't surprise Dina in the slightest, but it had come as a shock to run into him on the same errand as herself. She felt his tallness beside her, that power he had of making everything seem more significant, as if like some alchemist he threw a spell over the day. She felt the vitality and the challenge ... the sense of threat as Raf Ventura crossed her path once more.

She hoped that after they had concluded their business in the shop he would allow her to go home ... as she examined her satin slippers she was intensely aware of his scrutiny, and her nerves jumped when he took one of the slippers into his lean dark hand and quirked a look at her face.

Dina didn't dare to meet his eyes and was glad when the slippers were wrapped in their tissue paper and carefully placed in a white box so she could take them home with her.

'You have to see about your boots, so I'll be off——'

'Have tea with me—please?'

Never before in their association had he used that word and it caught at Dina, and this time she

149

did meet his eyes and they had a deep stillness to them, a waiting quality, as if he expected a refusal and would accept it if she chose to make it.

'I promised to go straight home,' she said, but as the cynicism stole back into his grey eyes she was sharply struck by the awareness that this might be their final chance to be together, for once she was married there could be no more meetings with him.

'All right,' she added. 'I—I am rather thirsty.'

'*Grazie.*' That was all he said, with not a hint of a smile on his face. He turned his attention to his riding-boots, long and supple, with an ox-blood gleam to the leather from which they were cut. He ran his lean hand over the leather, and Dina felt the tightening of tiny nerves in the region of her ribs. It was a tingling sensation, tipped by tiny barbs of fire, and she wasn't so naïve that she didn't know what caused the feeling as she gazed at that tapering hand like a swordsman's, with the speckless trimmed fingernails and none of that showy liking for rings on his fingers. What had he been in a previous existence? A sorcerer, or the son on the bar sinister side of a noble escutcheon?

As he stood there running a critical eye over those handmade boots he had more than a hint of the ruthless patrician in his profile; more of an air than those young men who formed part of the upper-crust of Californian society.

'What do you think?' He turned to her with a quick smile. 'A bit on the dashing side, eh, for a hotel-keeper?'

'They're like the boots of a *condottiere*,' she said.

'A soldier of fortune, eh? I suppose you could say I'm a modern version of one.'

They left the shop with their packages and outside on the pavement, in the sane light of the somewhat misty day, Dina was nervously tempted to say she had changed her mind about having tea with him. She cast a quick look at him and the breath caught in her throat, for he seemed to be reading her mind as his eyes raked over her face and ran down her slim body, clad in a suede hip-jacket, tapering check trousers, and a soft shirt almost the exact colour of her eyes. In the lobes of her ears were a tiny pair of cloudy ambers, and the opaque sunlight played over her silvery cap of hair.

'How devilishly pretty you are,' he almost growled. 'You are a rare creature, Dina Caslyn.'

'Oh—why?' A warmth swept upwards over her cheekbones, and a pulse beat quickly at the base of her throat. Nothing could be more dangerous than to be thought attractive by this man ... nothing could be more foolish than to stay and be aware that she wanted the bittersweetness of this meeting to be prolonged. Wanted it like an addict needing the wine that left a guilty hangover.

'You,' he shrugged, 'have a pair of perfect ears. Haven't you noticed, not many people have?'

'Raf——'

'You dare say it, what I see written in your eyes.' His eyes became a glittering grey and his jaw had set like iron. 'You can leave your car where you have parked it and we'll drive in mine to the place I have in mind for our tea. Is it so much to ask, when Bay Bigelow will be having you for breakfast, dinner and supper?'

'Is it wise?' she murmured.

'That, Dina, whether you realise it or not in your infinite innocence, is a provocative remark.'

His lips quirked. 'If you need to question the wisdom of being alone with me—my dear, the last time it was I who got the knee.'

'You don't forget, or forgive too easily, do you, Raf?'

'That?' A sudden brilliant amusement filled the depths of his eyes. 'I still have a very Italian soul, Dina, and I have no time for women of loose morals. It hurt like hell, but I deserved it. Good for you, but *dio mio*, how slim legs have sharp knees!'

'Raf, you could have killed me!'

'At that precise moment. Come, my car is just around this corner and I'll lug you there underneath my arm if you won't walk.'

Her fingers clenched the ribbon of her slipper box. An ordeal of uncertainty was hers—to go or not to go. Raf took a threatening step towards her, so tall as she looked up at him, dark-avised, lean and sinister, and supremely capable of carrying out his threat.

Dina walked with him to his car, feeling there was a minor earth tremor going on under her legs. He ran a large Hispano-Suiza from other days, bold coloured, outlandish, and remarkably well sprung. They drove along the Sunset Boulevard into the cool canyons of Beverly Hills, and came out upon the wide smooth road that led into Las Palmas.

Behind the wheel of the big car Raf was a clean and sweeping driver who cornered superbly. Dina knew in what direction they were heading, but at this stage there seemed no point in resisting him. They were on their way to his Sun Tower.

'You are as nervous as a kitten on the wrong side of the fence,' he said. 'Relax and you'll enjoy the ride—I'm not kidnapping you, as tempting as the idea might seem. Did you know that in certain parts of Italy if there is parental objection to a love match, then the young man snatches the girl and rides off with her. After they have spent a night together there can be no more objection to the match and so they are married in order to restore the girl's good name. Do you think such a system would work in America?'

Dina shot a glance at his profile and wondered if he were being cynical or serious. 'I wouldn't advise you to try it on,' she replied. 'American girls aren't quite so—so romantic, if that is the word for what happens in your wild Italian hills.'

'Doesn't such an elopement seem romantic to you?' He shot her a quizzing look. 'Are you so fearfully keen on all the rigmarole and ritual of so-called civilised marriage? There's a lot of reserve to you, Dina, and somehow I can't imagine that you like the idea of being the satin-clad star of a big production wedding to which many people have been invited, with buckets of champagne, dozens of presents, avid eyes on you from the moment you take your place beside the groom, looking like a lovely ghost. I believe you'd like to dash off to some quiet border town and get it all over as soon as possible. Come, am I right?'

'I'm sure you think you are,' she said, trying to speak distantly, in fear that he might read deeper into her mind ... and her heart.

'I was watching your face when you were shown your wedding slippers. Was that the smile of Cinderella that I saw, that tortured little twist of the lips?'

'You have a vivid imagination, Raf, and the Latin gift for making mystery where there is none.'

'I see. You have no confidante but your own heart, eh?'

'I'd hardly make a confidante of you,' she rejoined.

'I wonder why not when I also possess the Latin love of secrecy. Are there things in your heart, Dina, that I mustn't be told?'

'My heart, *signore*, is my affair, and if you're going to act the inquisitor then I'm going to insist that you turn the car and take me back to where I can pick up my coupé.'

'Ah, was it an unspoken covenant that you and I took tea together if I made polite conversation and kept my toes off your green-green grass? How boring, Dina. How tiresome to be barred from the naughtiness of saying forbidden things—after all, who is to know?'

'I shall know.'

'Isn't that carrying virtue a little too far? I'm sure your worthy young man can pot a shot with no touble at all, but I doubt his ability to read a woman's mind—least of all your mind, Dina.'

'I haven't a devious mind, thank you, nor one that is black as the inside of a tinker's kettle.'

'*Ouch*,' he laughed softly. 'Does Bay Bigelow know that you have a touch of temper and a shrewish little tongue at times? No, of course he doesn't! He barely knows a thing about the real you. He'd be shocked to his upstanding backbone if he even suspected that his snow-maiden could blaze into fury and know exactly where to disarm a man. Ah, what a waste of potential! As a man of business I hate to see anything at half capacity.'

'Thanks,' she said. 'If my voltage is that low, then I daresay you'll be glad to get back to the type of women who smoulder more than I do ... once you've satisfied your curiosity about me. Did you hope that I'd have one mad fling before my marriage—with you?'

'Heaven forbid that I'd be that fortunate.' As he spoke he swung the car on to the forecourt of his hotel, a grand sweep of a *piazza* fronting the towering façade of what he had visualised and had built to his exact requirements. His silver castle, thought Dina, as she climbed from the car and stood there gazing up at the glittering structure whose upper towers were lost in the mist. The last time she had been here she had been companioned by Bella and she hadn't known that the place was owned and run by Raf Ventura. She hadn't dreamed that he had watched her and wondered if she might be the type to have an affair with him.

She turned to face him ... her heart seemed to check as she met his eyes, almost crystalline in his lean dark face.

'What you're thinking isn't true at all,' he said harshly. 'I envied the all-American guy who might have you for his own, but I never thought for one minute that you went in for flings—last-minute or otherwise. You know, it might take the hook out of my throat if I could believe you were like so many other women, careless about cheating, corruptible, grabbing at today and not caring about tomorrow. But it looks as if I'm going to have to swallow that hook, or choke on it.'

'Don't talk like that.' She gave a little shiver and stared at his strong brown throat in the opening of his brown silk shirt. 'Are we going to the restaurant?' She made as if to cross to where a marble staircase led to the lobby, with its Persian blue chairs and carpet, its walls hung with an Italian harlequinade which she remembered studying. Had he watched her then? And what was it he had really hoped for?

His fingers caught her by the wrist. 'My penthouse—don't refuse, *donna mia*. You'll be as safe as Beatrice with Dante. I take my oath!'

His touch was warm against her skin, more surely intimate than anything had ever been. Fair Beatrice and dark Dante, meeting on a bridge that symbolised the separate lives that they would lead, chained hearts in bodies that walked apart.

'All right,' Dina murmured, and he escorted her to the scenic elevator of the hotel, a curving structure of glass and steel, winging them to his penthouse apartment at the very crown of the building. The mist closed around them, and she felt as if an eagle had hold of her and was carrying her into the sky.

They crossed a small lobby of golden polished wood and he unlocked a door into a spacious lounge whose parquet floor was covered here and there by rough wool rugs; the kind that he might have brought back from an Italian holiday. She saw a pair of enormous couches in off-white hide, hand-chiselled cabinets of dark glossy mahogany, and there on the wall a striking death-mask in bronze, with the satiny finish of perfect casting.

She didn't need to ask to whom the Italianate features had belonged; those lips that took the same mordant twist as Raf's when he was being cynical.

She felt him at the back of her, just close enough to be felt with every nerve in her body. 'Yes, Don Cicero,' he murmured. 'You see my facial likeness to my notorious grandparent, don't you? Are you wondering again if that resemblance is more than skin deep? If I am a member of the rackets and from them have made my money? This is what the godmother has planted in your head, eh, about me? Do you believe her?'

'No.' Dina made the decision suddenly and finally. 'I think you have a tough and ruthless brain, and you prefer the challenge of making your money rather than stealing it. Also your mother and father were hurt by the notoriety of—him.' She gestured at the bronze mask. 'Why was it made, and why do you have it on your wall?'

'My father had it done at the request of Don Cicero, to always remind me, his grandson, that crime leads nowhere in the end, only to death. It was a pity he ever left Italy. Does he seem to you to have the face of an infidel?'

'No, but faces can be deceptive, can't they?'

'You find my face that of a deceiver?' He placed his hands upon her shoulders and swung her to face him. She gazed up at him and he seemed to her to have the face of a conqueror, with the hair that slashed downwards on his forehead in an explicit black peak, with the bold Roman nose, and the jaw which had a keen, ruthless strength about it. He had no illusions about his own dynamic powers; he had never needed to be a member of a mob. He stood alone, and his Sun Tower was his symbol of himself.

'You are solitary, aren't you?' she said. 'Like the eagle, and this is your eyrie.'

'*Benvenuto!* Welcome to my eyrie.' He led her across the room and opened the glass doors of his private *terrazza*, where on a clear day a panorama of Las Palmas would be visible, and in the evening there would be a fantasy of lights and shadows, like being trapped in a beautiful glass bottle.

'You are still very nervous,' he said, quirking an eyebrow. 'Don't you like it on my side of the fence?'

'We both know that I'm playing truant, don't we, Raf?' She gazed out at the swirls of mist and felt on the edge of a precipice, let alone a fence.

'We met by chance,' he reminded her. 'We didn't plan to meet like guilty conspirators.'

'Isn't chance the fool's name for fate?' she asked. 'There is something fateful in the way we meet a—and it frightens me. I shouldn't have come here—I should have resisted when you asked.'

'Fate doesn't always permit us to resist. Let me take your coat.'

He had made up his determined mind that she would stay, so with tremulous fingers she unbuttoned her jacket and handed it to him. As his *terrazza* was completely enclosed by glass there was no sense of chill up here, even though the graceful building seemed to soar into the clouds.

'Won't you miss this when you move into your haunted mansion?' she asked.

'It will not look haunted when the builders and decorators are finally finished with it. In any case, I shall probably only use it for my rural base and will still spend most of my time here at the penthouse—did you think I had made plans to become a family man?'

'Would that be so surprising?' She made herself meet his eyes. 'Even an eagle must one day share his feathered nest—isn't it the law of nature?'

'Very much so, if he finds the mate to suit him.

Eagles can be obstinate when it comes to sharing their eyrie and if they can't find their chosen mate they prefer to fly alone.'

'Does that apply to Italian eagles? I thought it part of their natural heritage to want a son to follow them.'

'It is probably the heritage of most natural men, but I may have chained my desires to a very special kind of woman. Had you thought of that?' His scrutiny of her was quite unsparing as he spoke, and like an arrow it winged to her, that shattering sense of harmony that was totally unfelt with anyone else. With Raf she could say whatever came into her head, and it was a forbidden wine, an intoxicant she should run away from ... but where could she go? He had her trapped high above that other world where satin, silver and shining stones were being bonded together to make chains that would bind her to a socially desirable young man, whose heart was kind but whose eyes had never made her feel weak when he looked at her.

Grey and glittering eyes cutting away the silk shirt from her slim and virtuous body.

'Don't, Raf!' She gave him a faintly tortured look and his smile pursued her across the *terrazza*, where the high glass walls held her captive, like a moth in a bottle. 'You promised to be good.'

'I'm being a saint—for me.' His lean hand stole down the soft suede folds of her jacket, which he held over his arm. 'Take a seat while I phone down for tea—tell me, are you very hungry? I had to attend a board meeting and missed lunch and quite frankly I feel like having rather more than the traditional plate of cakes. What do you say?'

Dina had lunched sketchily herself, having been

too concerned for Bella to do more than peck at her food. There was rather an empty feeling at her midriff, and it also occured to her that if Raf were occupied with a good menu he might stop looking at her with those devouring eyes.

'I am rather peckish,' she admitted. 'What do you have in mind—in the way of food, I mean!'

'I bet at Satanita you don't often eat Italian.' His smile was raffish. 'I have an excellent chef, so will you leave the ordering to me?'

'I'll be glad to.'

'*Bene!* And do sit down and try to relax—standing like that you look rather like a butterfly which longs to make its escape.' He turned away and went into the lounge, crossing to the lobby out of her range of vision. Dina stood very still a moment and the silence seemed loud with the beating of her heart under the weightless silk of her shirt. She only wanted to go because she couldn't stay for ever, and feeling like a guilty prisoner she sank down into one of the Neptune chairs on the *terrazza*, of ivory woven cane with tiny gold patterns of stars and fishes around the high fans of the chairbacks.

Dina leaned back her head and closed her eyes and tried not to think of later on, when she had to face her godmother and provide a likely explanation for arriving home later than she had promised. She felt a stab of compunction when she thought of the redoubtable Bella laid low by one of her nerveracking headaches. Worrying about the wedding had brought it on; all that hectic attention to every tiny detail.

The wedding!

Dina clenched the armrests of the cane chair and

wished she could hide away and not have to be the 'star' attraction. How would she face all those people, and those flashlight bulbs that would light up her face and surely reveal the shadow that lurked in her eyes?

How could she cast out that tall, dark shadow?

The substance of that shadow came through the glass doors and stood looking down at her. 'I think this is the first time in days that you have sat down and not heard in your ears the infernal sound of women in a ferment of wedding hysteria. This is so, Dina?'

She moved her head in agreement, for there was no denying this sense she felt of being suspended in time and space, where no one could find her; where she could forget for a while that she wasn't free to be herself ... as Raf was free, would always be free, like an eagle.

'Like preparing Anne Boleyn for her walk to the block and the shining blade in the hand of the axe-man, eh?'

'Oh, not quite so fearful,' she protested. 'What a Borgia-like imagination you have, Raf! You see things in stark black and white, don't you?'

'Not entirely.' His eyes moved over her face and hair, which caught the strange opaque light through the windows of his eyrie. 'I also see gleams of silver and gold ... I think you and I will have a drink before our food arrives, a *vino nobile* which I have been saving for a special—friend.'

'A friendship that has to end in an hour,' she said.

'When the Snow Princess will have no more time for her knave?'

'I'm not a princess, nor are you a knave.'

'What am I, then?' He looked directly into her eyes, and she thought of her very first meeting with him and how wickedly sinister she had believed him to be. Anything could have been true of him, except the real truth ... that to those he loved he could be supremely generous, enough to let them leave him. His parents were in Italy. His sisters were scattered. He lived alone in his ivory tower.

'A lonely man,' she said. 'I bet your mother and father are always telling you to find a ravishing Italian girl to settle down with. I—I wish you would, Raf.'

'Do you really?'

'It's better than loneliness.'

'It's a loneliness we'll share.' He reached down, unclenched her hands from their hold on the arms of her chair and held them in his own hands. 'So I'm not to be a friend, not even that? A casual kind of uncle to your Bigelow babies?'

'Don't, Raf!'

'I shan't, but he will. You're on the block, Dina, and piece by piece you'll be hacked away until all that's left is your crying heart. You don't love the man who is going to own every living piece of you.'

She turned her head away, unable to meet his unsparing eyes. The silence swirled around them like the mist around the tower and she could feel his fingers tight around hers, and the pain of Bay's ring being pressed into her finger bone. She wanted to cry out in terror at the image he evoked, for she was one of those who had been born for only one man ... and that man wasn't Bay Bigelow.

'You don't love him, but that won't matter to all

those who make merry at the wedding and wish him joy of you.'

'It will make Bella happy—I owe her—so much.'

'To hell with Bella!'

'No.' Dina shook her head at him. 'I'd have been put into an institution if it hadn't been for her—my father became a hopeless drunk. I'd have had none of the things she gave me, my education, my clothes, my friends. It's a small price to pay.'

'And you'll never cease to pay it, you realise that, I suppose?'

'It won't be such a bad life——'

'Will it be a happy one?' he demanded. 'Holy heaven, will it be exciting and rewarding, something you'll want to wake up to, a joy you'll long to find when the darkness falls?'

'Is passion everything?' she asked quietly.

'Yes, if one has glimpsed it in a pair of eyes.'

'You think I have done so?'

'I don't think, *donna mia,* I happen to know.' With that he went into his sitting-room and distantly she heard the clink of glasses and knew he was pouring the wine. Dina looked beyond the *terrazza* windows and gave a little shiver; the mist seemed to press closer to the glass and tiny globules of moisture hung there like diamonds. The mystery and melancholy held her entranced, as if here with Raf she was stranded upon a mountain peak.

Oh, how easy it might be to hold fast to the strange dream, but all dreams had to give way to reality.

'The haze seems more intense,' she said, when Raf returned. 'I—I really must go in a while—it could turn into a smog.'

'I shall drive you,' he said. 'Don't worry—you'll

see hell and chivalry in my eyes before the day is over.'

She looked upwards into his eyes, clairvoyant as the edge of the descending axe on her slim neck. He bent and put into her hand a Verzelini goblet with golden patterns woven into the glass and set on a shining stem. The wine was a deep red, like rubies, like flame, like distilled passion.

'To think that a vineyard has to be ravaged to produce such a wine,' he said, and his smile twisted on the edge of his mouth, '*Salúte*.'

'*Salúte*.' The wine ran warm and potent down her throat, easing away that bruised feeling when she swallowed. Raf lounged by the *terrazza* wall, his profile outlined against the misty glass. The vapour seemed to be thickening with each passing moment, visibility was diminishing, and sounds from below were becoming indistinct. Across the water a fog-horn wailed, weird and almost animal, and more than ever they seemed detached from the rest of the world.

'You are very private and solitary up here, aren't you?' The wine had warmed her and created a sense of relaxation and the smile she gave him was in her eyes. 'Does it give you a feeling of power, prince of your very own castle, master of your destiny, the sorcerer in his citadel, plotting his next move in the complex game of high finance? Do you look out over Las Palmas and feel that you own your very own soul?'

'Something like that.' His eyes held hers. 'What of your soul, Dina? Is it in bondage?'

'No——'

'You can't pretend with me and you know it. You've known it from the beginning that we share a chemistry more potent, more magical, more stimulating than the headiest wine. Can you really turn your back on it to cleave to a mere boy, who will look upon you as just another useful and attractive possession, like his tennis rackets, his golf clubs, and his well-groomed polo ponies? You saw him matched against me on the tennis court and I made him look hot and harassed, eh? Believe me, *donna mia*, he has no idea how to handle a sensitive woman. He thinks it is just a matter of good manners and apologetic biology.'

'You've a clever tongue, Raf, but you won't sway me, conquer me, be my master—I won't let you!'

'What if you can't help yourself? Come, you knew me for your master from the first moment that our eyes met.'

'How arrogantly cocksure you are, Raf!' She tossed her head and played the game, for it was a game and could be nothing else. 'A master of words and women as well as financial wizardry. I know what you're trying to do, but it won't work.'

'What am I trying to do?' His smile was brief, a blade-edge of white teeth, a glittering of his eyes.

'Inflame my doubts, increase my fears, whisper like the devil in my ear. Stop it right now, Raf.'

'What will happen if I don't? Will I fall from grace?'

'I think you might.'

'In which case you will behold Satan falling like a bolt from the heavens—except that I've never been there. I've had only a stolen glimpse beyond the gates, and then an angel flashed her golden eyes and ordered me away.'

He lounged there, so free of anyone's domination, so relentlessly his own master, and then his voice dropped into a lower key. 'Why don't you stop being a martyr?' His tones were tigerish, as were his eyes. 'Start being a woman—a woman who wants a man, not a damned half-baked boy!'

'Want—take, ride life like a pirate!' Her eyes blazed back into his. 'I'm not you, Raf! You're pagan-hearted! You'd have me break promises, let people down, deny the duties I must fulfil in order to keep my pride. I've little else but that. It's a trifle saved over from my father's destruction of his life and himself.'

'All very noble, Dina, but you're going to be married against your deepest instincts, and nothing is harder on this earth for a woman than to give herself cold-hearted to a man.'

'I—I won't listen to you! I'll go, now——'

'You'll go nowhere, running away again from the raw truth. Dina, *donna mia*, you can't kick love aside, it's almighty tenacious and will grow like the olive tree among stones.'

'But it won't bear fruit,' she flung back at him.

'But it will bear memories, Dina, among its shaking silver leaves. Not you, not I, nor Bay Bigelow, can stop their growth, and you'd be amazed how vigorous memories can grow with the years, especially in the heart of a woman who has denied her true self, her own real destiny, and made of herself one of society's mechanical dolls, wound up in the morning on strong black coffee, reinforced mid-morning on a nip of best brandy, all smoothly oiled and blank-faced by the dinner hour or the bridge party, or the country club dance, having got herself hooked on Martinis or vodka.'

He spoke with a controlled violence, but it was

his eyes most of all that terrified Dina. They had gone molten silver in his dark face and the pupils held a pair of flames. Love! He had said the word at last and it had gone through her like a barb, fixing itself in her heart, causing a sharp and very personal pain. She didn't dare to love him ... only in the deep, secret recesses of her body and mind. Only there was it safe to rejoice that he did love her, a sweet and bitter joy that she could not reveal.

She didn't dare reveal it, neither trusting him nor herself should she find herself in his arms again. She had to hurt him ... there was no other way.

She had to find it in her to throw cold water on his ardency and watch the flames abruptly quenched in his fiery eyes. Those eyes that showed her that love could be a passionate wonder with no room for any of the tepid emotions that passed for love among certain of her friends. This she had to sacrifice in favour of a mere spark that lit no flame in her blood. This she had to quench when every particle of her longed to be melted in the fierce and glowing warmth of what Raf was offering her ... a rapture of the senses from which there would be no return to the sanity to which she must cling.

A flight with an eagle was not for her, and she braced herself for the conflict between love and duty.

CHAPTER SIX

'WHAT I choose to do with my life has nothing whatsoever to do with you,' she said to him. 'I came here because I didn't like to refuse you, but if you're going to rant and rave then I prefer to go home.' She rose to her feet as she spoke and went to sweep past him. He reached out, caught at her wrist and jarred the lovely goblet out of her grasp. It fell with a musical crash to the tiled floor of the *terrazza* and splintered into jewelled fragments. Raf stared a moment at the debris, then deliberately tossed down his own goblet, smashing it in the glittering shards of its twin.

'That's the traditional way to end a *passe d'armes*,' he drawled.

'Oh, what a pity,' she murmured. 'What a waste!'

'Symbolic, my dear. Let us go and eat.' He swept an arm about her waist and propelled her across the main room of the penthouse into a dining-room where a table had been perfectly laid for two, with butterfly orchids as a centrepiece.

'Stay, now everything is prepared,' he said, and when Dina saw a waiter by the side-table she made no further objection and slid into the chair which Raf drew out for her. If the waiter felt that this was an odd time of the day for Raf Ventura and his guest to be dining, it didn't show on his face. He gave a slight bow as he placed the napkin across her knees and proceeded to serve up the first course of large prawns baked in slices of lemon, served with fresh-baked rolls, a smooth mayonnaise, and a white wine.

'I can see to the rest, Salvatore,' Raf said to him. 'Thank the chef on my behalf, and take your siesta.'

'Si, signore. Grazie.'

The door closed, and Raf gazed across the orchids at Dina, lean fingers breaking a roll in half. 'Shades of the last supper, eh?'

She nodded and dipped a luscious prawn in the creamy sauce. 'You won't play Judas and betray me for trusting you?'

'I don't need the thirty pieces of silver, but I'd sell my soul to—no matter. You are fond of prawns?'

'Mmmm, these are excellent. Your staff are either terrified of you, or incredibly loyal, to produce a meal like this after a frantic morning serving the restaurant.'

'Which do you think it is, terror or loyalty?' His lips gave that characteristic quirk as he tossed a pink prawn between his teeth.

'A combination of both,' she decided. 'I think all your associations would be based on those two factors.'

'You make me sound feudal.'

'Aren't you?'

'Perhaps, in the sense that I take care of my own people and give the best service of which I'm capable. I have had to make the Ventura name respected and trustworthy, and I shall fight your godmother tooth and claw if she dares to dig up what I have successfully interred. As I once told you, the vendetta is in my blood and Bella Rhinehart will learn how to weep if she ever does anything to really infuriate me.'

'Don't, Raf!' Dina gave a little shiver at the look that came into his eyes. 'When you look like that you make my heart go cold. Wasn't it tempting providence to buy Adam's Challenge?'

'Your godmother doesn't own that select section of California where you live, Dina. In a sense none of us own anything, we are by the grace of the gods given the chance to make life satisfying for ourselves and at the end of it to take nothing with us but our souls and the possible love of another human being. I'm no saint, but by heaven there will be the devil to pay if that woman—ah, let's forget her for now!' He rose as he spoke, collected the empty plates and took them to the side-table. While he dished up their second course Dina let her eyes rove around his dining-room.

The chairs, tables and corner cabinets were in close-grained olive wood of a green-gold colour, and a pair of lovely old Venetian lamps hung from the ceiling. But what caught Dina's gaze and held it was a boldly painted wall panel of a classic scene which she suddenly realised was that of the god Perseus saving the rock-chained Andromeda from the dragon. There was a mingling of gold, flame, and satin-dark skin, and she was still looking at the panel when Raf placed a plate of food in front of her.

'It is eye-catching, is it not?' he drawled.

'Are you fond of the classic myths?' she asked.

'That particular one.' He sat down and readjusted his table napkin. 'Come, eat your *pasta* while it's really hot, before the cheese has a chance to set.'

Dina ate a forkful of the hot cheese and celery *pasta*, with a sauce of tomatoes, herbs and shrimp. It was delicious and obviously created by a real Italian cook.

'You don't have that served at Satanita, eh?' His smile was wicked. 'It is even better when enjoyed beside the Adriatic, with the sun on the water and the sound of Italian voices filling the air. The joy of living, and loving, is something very rich in my people.'

'Tell me about Italy,' she said, feeling it would be a safer subject than anything else ... all other channels of conversation seemed to lead into dangerous waters, and her eyes flicked from his lean features to those of the young god who fought to snatch Andromeda from the dragon. Nothing was insignificant where Raf was concerned. He made her aware of herself as no one had ever done ... made each moment in his company a tiny drama in itself.

'Have you never been there, Dina?'

'I shall be going——' She broke off and dabbed sauce from the corner of her mouth ... it had happened again, without warning they were back in the cross tides.

'On your honeymoon, eh?' He gave a short laugh. 'I expect the bridegroom will show you all the four-star places marked in the tourist guide book and you will come home to America believing you have seen Italy.'

'There's no need to be sarcastic, Raf.'

'It amuses me, the American conception of seeing a foreign country. It's like a mad dash round an obstacle course and so long as the obvious places are seen and quickly ticked off on the itinerary it

171

doesn't seem to worry the breathless tourist that the most intriguing mountain villages are never seen, where a lot of the old ways are still intact and have not lost their strange charm. Will you be visiting Venice—the perfect city for lovers?'

'That will be up to Bay,' she said, fixing her eyes upon her plate of *pasta*.

'I see, so you plan to be the perfectly obedient bride, following meekly in your husband's footsteps?'

'Isn't that your conception of what a wife should be?' He had put a spark to her temper, as he had probably meant to, and when Dina met his eyes she found them amused ... and yet also faintly shadowed, or was that just the effect of Italian eyes, sheltered as they were by those thick black lashes?

'The Latin takes a mate and he hopes that like the female jaguar she will be loyal to him alone, a clawing, spitting fury to any other male. The jaguar is no tame creature, Dina, crawling on its gold belly in the grass, purring all the time, running for cover if its mate should snarl and growl. They fight, and by the gods, how they love!'

Dina stared into his eyes and saw there a fierce, beckoning flame. It blazed up, then sank down, and she saw his face contort as if in pain. 'Oh, Raf,' his name was a soft, broken cry. 'If you care, then don't make things harder for me——'

'So you admit that it isn't going to be easy?' He bit out the words with his hard white teeth.

'Is anything easy in this life?' she asked. 'I wish to heaven I had never met you! Why—why did you have to come and speak to me?'

'Law of the jungle, Dina. I saw my equal, my match, and if all I was to have was a snatch of conversation, then I'd have it. I'd have more—everything, but you're so damnably straight and I don't want to break your spirit. You're such a—a thoroughbred, and one doesn't use a whip or a spur on you.'

She sat silent, moving a piece of shrimp around her plate with her fork. She loved him, then, as never before. Not because of what he thought of her, but because he held his hand and kept control of what smouldered in his eyes.

'It's ironic, is it not?' His smile was infinitely sombre. 'That an Italian should fall hopelessly in love with a girl of a different race, religion and class. My parents would be shocked, my sisters sceptical, and my priest would advise caution, but I would disregard them all if I could have you without hurting you. I've never felt this way before—protective of a woman and possessive at the same time. This should have happened to me when I was a youth. Calf love can be painful, but it isn't incurable.'

Dina didn't want to be thrilled by his words, but they did thrill her, tightening her skin and making it tingle. No one would ever have for her the strange magic that Raf had, and yet she had to deny it and walk away from him. She owed too much to Bella, and Raf was strong enough to forget her and find someone else to take her place.

'Your parents would be right to be shocked,' she said. 'You love and admire your own kind of people ... whatever we feel it was never meant to be. A brief interlude, Raf. A few bars of music snatched in the air. Let it be that way, with no regrets.'

'Don't be so sure about the regrets,' he said, a

little harshly. 'I have you here with me now, and it won't be easy to let you go.'

'But you will let me go?'

'I can't be sure, *donna mia*. There's a devil in me.'

'But you're in control of it.'

'At this moment, Dina, but what will happen when I have to open my door to let you out of my life?' His eyes held hers, a stern kind of gravity in them. 'Will you take dessert?'

'Dessert?'

'It's something a little special. *Cassata*, an ice-cream *bombe* of cream and fruit encased in whipped cream.'

'It sounds delicious, Raf.'

He sat there looking at her, slowly moving his eyes over her face, her hair, the amber-stoned lobes of her ears, the slim length of her neck. 'For me that term applies to you——'

'Raf, you're breaking that promise you made!'

'I'm not touching you, I am merely looking.'

'A—a look from you is all it takes, and you know it!'

'You're trembling—ah, Dina, why deny me, yourself—you want me to touch you with more than my eyes? You ache and hurt with it as I do, and by the saints, I am not made of martyr substance even if you are!' Back went his chair, skidding and crashing sideways on the parquet floor. A couple of impetuous strides and he was by her side, reaching for her, the heat of his hands through the fine silk of her shirt. She heard his throaty whisper and felt the warm crush of his arms. At the touch of his lips on hers a flame shot through her blood and her response to him was like the shaking of a lamp

174

which had burned with a still and constant light until this moment.

For a single wild moment she resisted him, and then to be this close to what she must surrender was too much for her and she allowed her lips, her heart, her very bones to fill with love of him. They clung fiercely, like two people on the deck of a sinking ship ... like lovers kissing goodbye before plunging from a burning building.

Her fingers sank deep into his black hair, holding him as he held her, as if there were no tomorrow ... and for them it was bleakly true, there was nothing beyond these breathless moments, their bodies locked as their souls were locked.

Dina hadn't known that the body could come alive like this ... to such an unbearable pitch that they wrenched apart in the same instant, staring at each other with tormented eyes.

'Let me love you,' he groaned.

'No—oh no, Raf. There'd be no strength, no will to leave, and I have to leave—you.' She turned and ran into the sitting-room, where her legs went weak as water so that she half fell on to the nearest couch, burying her face in her hands. Her shoulders trembled when his touch came, down over her flesh and bones, a part of her so that she wanted to reach out for his hand and pull it to her heart ... the heart she gave to *il tigre* in the body she must deny him. If he took her body he took everything and she had a debt of pride and honour to repay.

'It hurts like hell itself.' His fingers crushed the silk that covered her. 'You're mine and I won't give you up! Why should I? I have every right to what cleaves to me, burns for me, as I burn. You're ice—

sheer frozen ice for any other man, and you know it!'

'Take me home,' she pleaded. 'I—I can't bear any more.'

'Your home is where I am.' His hand wrapped itself about her neck and he forced her to look at him. His eyes poured down into her a kind of scalding incandescence of love and desire ... a worship and a wanting that she would never see again beyond this moment. Raf, loving for the first time as she loved ... loving for the last time, as she did.

'Have a little mercy on me, darling Raf,' she whispered. 'You said I was straight, you said I had a certain virtue—if it was those qualities that moved you and made you care for me, then don't ask me to bend them and tarnish them.'

'Why should I care, if I have you?' he growled.

'You'd have the body, but would you have the soul? Would you have that, Raf, if you made me—made me give myself?'

'It would be something,' he half snarled. 'What shall I have if I let you go out of here, to him, with nothing for myself? I have my feelings, Dina. I'm not a damned robot!'

'I have feelings as well—do you think I haven't?' Suddenly her eyes filled with tears, and she longed with every particle of herself to reach up and take his lean, love-twisted face into her hands. She wanted to kiss his eyes and lose herself in the molten hunger of his hard lean body ... but for the guilt afterwards, and the haunting fear of what Bella might have the power to do to him. She had friends in high places, and Raf's past as the grand-son of a notorious criminal could be raked up and

176

the shining life he had made for himself in America could be smeared and ruined ... these things could be done so easily, and Dina had always known that her godmother was a ruthless woman ... far more ruthless than Raf would ever be.

Raf, who loved her. She knew it more certainly than she had ever known anything. She felt it, reaching out like a living thing, fine and strong, and not to be broken even when she wrenched herself apart from him.

'Couldn't you be a lesser woman?' he groaned. 'Why do you have to be one hell of an angel? I never wanted an angel—I only asked for a mate to share with me the things I've worked for.'

'You'll find her, Raf, and you'll make a good life for yourself, fulfilled and warm with good things— children——' She broke off, unable to suppress a gasp of pain from inside her, and from without, for his hands were suddenly biting into her shoulders, unaware or uncaring that they were cruel in their strength and their passion.

'I want your children,' he said, his voice deep and harsh. 'Made with you and born from your body and heart. I'll have no others, I take my oath on that! No son, no daughter, unless you give them to me. Don't you understand yet? I love you, utterly, completely, with my bones, my body, my brain. If I can't have you, then I'll have nothing and nobody! That's the way I am made, Dina. All or nothing.'

And there was no doubting what he said. His face was drawn into harsh lines of pain, and his eyes had gone dark with it. He looked as a man would look when being tortured, in a kind of ecstasy of agony. It was almost frightening for

Dina, to see him like this, he who had been like a solitary eagle flying in arrogant aloofness and sureness, his very own master.

Now he was mastered by what he felt for her, and every instinct in Dina wanted to respond to him, in pity and passion; in love and longing.

'I—I'm desperately sorry, Raf.' It was all she could manage to say, and she knew how inadequate the words sounded, for she couldn't speak aloud what lay in her heart. She didn't dare reveal the depth and torment of her own suffering . . . no pain had ever been this personal, deep down in those secret recesses that were the very woman of her. She clamoured to be close to this man and to never know again what it felt like to be apart from him, but stronger than desire was her need to make him safe from any kind of vengeance. Because he loved her, he didn't deserve to have his life wrecked. Dina couldn't endure the thought of it. He had worked long and hard, and he had buried the past. It must stay buried, and if that was all she could give him, then she would give it with both hands and with all her heart.

'Don't they say *che será, será* in Italy?' she asked. 'Whatever will be, will be? You knew when you first spoke to me that I wasn't—free.'

'I knew of your engagement—when we spoke together I knew you didn't love the man whose ring you wore. I looked into your eyes, Dina, and I saw there the loneliness that a mutual love would long since have shut out of your life. To find such a love is never to be lonely, even when you're apart from the one who wants you, needs you—as the body the fresh air, and the warm sun. That is why I approached you, why I spoke to you. I was curious to see if you carried in your eyes the unmistakable love light, but instead I saw only the cool golden beauty of your gaze and I knew that you were to be sacrificed on the altar of a socially desirable marriage. You will never know how fierce was my inclination to carry you off with me, away from people who regard themselves as the epitome of civilised living and yet who live by the rules of old Roman society, ancient Greek law, when the young and lovely were either forced into vestal virginity, or married off into wealthy households regardless of their personal desires.

'Ah, Dina,' his voice sank down as he knelt beside the couch where she sat, and he reached for her hand and she knew that it was an object of ice in his warm fingers ... so warm, so strong, so vital with life. She looked at him and in the strange light filtering into the room from windows that seemed hung with a fine impenetrable gauze, his face seemed to her like those faces of gothic knights seen in the tinted windows of Cistercian chapels. And it was the chivalry in him to which she had to appeal.

'If you truly care for me, Raf, then be understanding of what I must do. It's my cross, and I don't want you to speak of being alone yourself. I—I couldn't bear that. You weren't made for it.'

'No,' he agreed, the faintest hint of irony stealing back into his eyes. 'I haven't the temperament of a monk, but nature made me choosy and I don't think I could ever find another girl who is just like *cassata*, a delicious mixture of hot and cold, all wrapped up in a pure creamy skin. *Cristo santo*, I can't be near you and not—not——' He leapt to his feet, vibrant as a dangerous animal driven to the very edge of an attack.

He stood very still, gazing tensely at the mist-shrouded windows of his penthouse. All sound was curiously muffled, and there seemed to be a tint of flame beyond the mist.

'The sun is going down,' he murmured, 'and the city is drowned in the vapour. You must eat *cassata* with me, and then I'll take you home—if that is what you want me to do?'

Dina didn't dare to contemplate what she truly wanted ... merely to look at him was to feel a clutch of excitement and doom. 'I—I don't think I could manage another bite——'

'Try,' he urged. 'Let me pretend just this once that I share a real Italian sweet with you on some very secluded beach where afterwards you would lie in my arms and not use the tricks of judo on my defenceless anatomy.'

He gave a slight laugh and went into the dining-room. Dina got quickly to her feet, snatched up her handbag and the box which held her wedding slippers, and made for the door that led out to the lobby. Her heart was hammering. She had to reach the elevator before Raf heard her, and once she was downstairs she could hail a cab and be away ... not looking back in case it hurt too much and made her cry out.

She was halfway across the lobby when the telephone rang. The sudden clamour of it made her nerves leap as if they were on wires and the shoe-box fell from her hand. In a fever of trepidation Dina grabbed up the box and ran to the lift.

'Don't!' he cried out behind her. He had heard the phone and had come hurrying to answer it. 'Dina—please!'

It was a command and a painful appeal, and she stood there like someone teetering on the edge of a dark pit. The button that would summon the lift was just there beyond her reaching hand, and she had to force herself to touch that button with enough strength to bring the lift to the penthouse floor.

Beyond the lobby of Raf's apartment she heard him speaking on the phone, crisply, his voice as incised as words on metal. Still her heart was pounding as if she had been running and she put a hand against her throat and prayed for the lift to arrive before he finished his conversation.

'You won't go—not now!' He was striding across to her and she swung round to confront a face turned to stone, in which his eyes held a terrible blaze. Dina backed away from him, hearing the swish of the lift doors opening behind her just as Raf caught roughly hold of her.

'You're staying—with me. Nothing, nobody, can now do a thing about it. I'm claiming what is mine!'

'Raf, you must let me go! Please, don't make a scene!' She struggled with him, but with arrogant strength he swept her up into his arms and carried her back into his penthouse, leaving behind them the gaping doors of the elevator. His arms were like bands of steel around her and he held her with a force that she couldn't fight.

'Raf,' instinct directed her words, 'who was that on the phone?'

'The fire chief of the Pasadena fire-fighting brigade.' He gazed down at her, holding her eyes with his. 'Adam's Challenge has been burned to the ground and they caught the arsonist immediately afterwards—a bit of a boy who was paid to set fire to my property. The police aren't gentle with fire-raisers and they managed to get from him the name of the person who hired him to do the job.'

Raf paused and Dina saw a cruel twist of anger on his lips. He held her bruisingly close to him and she felt the hard pounding of his heart through the material of his brown shirt.

'It seems that your godmother telephoned Royal and Weale to ask if you had called in—they said you had, in the company of a Signor Ventura. Enough said, eh? Bella Rhinehart then made a second call from her sickbed, and a short time later my house became a flaming inferno, as it would be with cans of paint and cleaning fluid on the premises. Thanks to mercy the workmen had left for the day!'

No! Dina wanted to deny his allegation that Bella was involved in anything so shocking. She moistened dry lips, but the words wouldn't come. In her mind's eye she saw the flames against the night sky, heard the roar of falling timbers, saw the portrait of the Penrose girl fall from the wall into the greedy, consuming heat. Gone was the fair ghost, and Raf's dream of turning that old house back into a real home ... somewhere he could go when the pressures of his work built up.

Oh God, she didn't want to believe that Bella could arrange such a revenge, not when she had left her on a bed of pain...

And had promised to be home just as soon as the final fitting of the wedding dress had taken place!

'You are not going back to that woman.' Raf spoke decisively, his mouth grim, his eyes dominating Dina. 'You are staying here with me, where

182

you belong. Now you see to what extremes she will go to have her own way. She gave to you with one hand, and with the other she underlined your duty to repay her for every tiny favour. This she has drilled into you until you hardly knew if you were living her life or your own.

'Now,' his eyes became exultant, 'now she has set you free by her own egotistical hand. Now you will live your own life—with me!'

Dina heard him as in a kind of dream. Her head drooped against his shoulder. Was it remotely possible that she could do as he said, cast free her chains and stay with him in love and honour?

'No,' she murmured, 'I have to speak with her. I have to hear what she has to say. I—I can't not go back—don't you see?'

'I see only your white face and your big eyes. I know only that I want to protect you from her.' He lowered Dina to a couch and sat beside her, holding her hands and chafing some warmth back into them. 'You must have a brandy to take away the shock.'

'Oh, Raf, what could have induced her to do such a thing?' Dina's eyes clung to his and all she could think of was that her deepest fears had been realised. Because of her Raf was in danger. Because she was here with him, his house had been burned down.

'It's because I love you,' he said, leaning forward to kiss her pale cheek. 'Because you love me. There are people who have never known it and she is one of them, and I think she made up her mind long ago that you were going to be used to pay back Lewis Caslyn for turning his back on her and walking into the ocean. Tell me now, Dina, will you exchange what I hold out to you for what she has given with the cold and calculating heart of a woman bent on seeing you as unhappy in your marriage as she was in hers? Her husband died a strange death—did he fall or was he pushed?'

Raf rose to pour brandy into a pair of bowls, and Dina sat there and absorbed his words ... the terror in them, and the possible terrible truth. He came back to her and placed one of the stemmed bowls in her hand.

'Drink it and you will feel better.'

She drank and felt the warmth stealing back into her body. 'What will happen, Raf?' she murmured. 'Will there be—trouble?'

'Yes. It can't be avoided as the youth was caught —as these people sometimes are, being unable to resist the fascination of the fire they create.'

'Oh, what am I to do?' Dina wrapped her hands about the brandy bowl and stared into it as if seeking some answer to her cry. 'I grew up in her house. I was treated like her daughter—and there's Bay! He doesn't deserve to be hurt by all this.'

'Do I, Dina?'

She glanced up at Raf and there sprang into her eyes a quick flame of compassion, and love. 'No, not you—not you! But it must be done with honesty and honour, Raf. I must see both of them. I can't just walk out.'

'You follow the straight road all the way, don't you, *carissima*?' Raf sat down at her side and he smiled at her with a shattering gentleness. 'I can afford to be generous, I think, if I am to have at last the dream and the reality in the shape of my Dina. I love you with all my heart, my dearest dear. I love your sense of pride and honour. I love your

184

eyes and the feel of your hand in mine. I shall be a man so much in love that my parents will forget to be disapproving and they, too, will take you to their hearts. I wonder, would you like to live in Italy with me?'

'With you, dear Raf? Far away from all you have built? Your sun tower, for instance?' Dina reached out to touch his face, running her fingers down the line of his hard jaw. 'Would you want that?'

'With you, Dina, anywhere would be heaven, and what is a sun tower by comparison to a towering love? Finish your brandy and we will face the dragon—together.'

But it wasn't to be that Dina would ever confront her godmother again. After that long and hazardous drive through the thick mist, that clung in tear-shaped globules to the windows of the car, they arrived at Satanita to find Bella in a coma. She didn't awake from that last sleep, self-induced by a certain drug, but she left a letter for Dina; and it simply said:

'I couldn't bear it that any man should take Lewis's daughter away from me. Bay would not have done so, but Raffaello Ventura will have all of you. He meant to on the morning he rode into my garden like a black angel on horseback. I have hated him even as I have watched you grow to love him. I wish he could have been at Adam's Challenge when it went up in flames. I'd like him to burn in hell, but instead he'll be with you—love is heaven, I suppose.'

Raf read the letter without saying a word, then he placed it on a table and involuntarily they walked out together into the dawn-lit garden, from which the mist was lifting to reveal the shapes of the trees.

Breaking their news to Bay lay ahead of them, but with Raf's strong arm around her Dina knew that she could face the world. She flung up her head and looked at him ... yes, she had known intuitively that the strands of her life would become interwoven with his, creating a design that her godmother would find disastrous. It had been fated to happen that way, and because Dina was generous she would remember the good times at Satanita and gradually she would forget the last sad moments of being here.

Today she would go with Raf to the sun tower, to book in there as a guest until they had a licence and could drive off quietly to be made man and wife.

So would it be, and she stood there, folded into his arms as the sun rose over the treetops. As the day brightened and the dark shadows retreated, Dina drew a deep breath and felt Raf's arms tighten around her.

'Time will mend the memories,' he murmured. 'I will see to it, my darling, believe me.'

'I do—utterly.' She turned to him, knowing his need of her to be as strong as her need for him. It would, after all, be a fine romance, with many, many kisses.

'Oh—Raf!' Her breath was lost in the warmth of his loving mouth. All doubts were gone as the sun broke into a golden blaze.

Best Seller Romances

Romances you have loved

Mills & Boon Best Seller Romances are the love stories that have proved particularly popular with our readers. They really are "back by popular demand." These are the other titles to look out for this month.

THERE CAME A TYRANT
by Anne Hampson

Simoni knew she would just never get on with Kent Travers. He was tyrannical, unreasonable, for ever finding fault with her and her work. Thank goodness they would both soon be leaving their jobs and she need never have anything to do with him again. But that was where Simoni was wrong!

INNOCENT DECEPTION
by Rachel Lindsay

Sharon had had no ulterior motive when she took on the job of looking after Paul Sanderson's small daughter – but if he knew who she was, he would be certain to suspect her of one. So she must be careful to keep her identity a secret. She must be even more careful not to fall in love with him . . .

Mills & Boon

COME RUNNING
by Anne Mather

Darrell Anderson had fallen in love with Matthew Lawford, who was married – unhappily, but married none the less. She knew that she would still go to him on any terms he chose to name – but was there any chance of happiness for them, even if she did?

ADAM'S RIB
by Margaret Rome

Tammy Maxwell and Adam Fox had married for nothing but expediency – and now here she was, installed in his remote house in the Cumbrian Fells; realising, too late, that she had fallen in love with him – and that he felt nothing for her but contempt. What should she do now?

FLIGHT INTO YESTERDAY
by Margaret Way

To Lang Frazer, Natalie was just a spoilt, heartless girl who revelled in hurting her father and her stepmother Britt. But Natalie saw Britt as the woman who had ruined her relationship with her father. How could she see Lang with anything but resentment? What did he know about it all anyway?

the rose of romance

ROMANCE